Puffin Books
Editor: Kaye Webb

Eusebius the Phoenician

'I seek not the praise of warrior or gods,' Eusebius the Phoenician merchant told his bewildered Viking hosts. 'That is no prize which I would value. What I have come here for is far beyond that in worth.

'Of all the wonders that the Israelites are known to have performed there is one that interests me especially, and that is the bringing of a man back from the dead. It is said that this man was able to raise himself from the dead as a result of drinking from a particular Cup which he had. He said that those who drank from that Cup would never die. I seek the Cup.'

'I have never heard of this Cup,' said Sigurd. 'But if you wish to journey to the White Island, I will give you a ship and men and a pilot and you will be at liberty to go there and seek your Cup of Life.'

Thus it was that Eusebius and his Viking crew set forth for the White Island, named from the white cliffs of Dover, on the strangest journey in their lives, one on which they were to meet the aged King Arthur at his empty Round Table and travel westwards through the perilous Forest of Eppin, the Great Plain of the Stones, through the Singing Hills and the Western Wilderness, and so to the lake in which lay Avalon, and the mystical discovery that Eusebius had been half expecting all along.

This is an exhilarating, richly imaginative book about a time when the most ordinary things were endowed with a magic, mystery and awe that has been worn away in succeeding generations until our own more prosaic age.

For readers of eleven and over.

Cover design by Richard Kennedy

Eusebius
The Phoenician

Christopher Webb

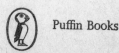 Puffin Books

Puffin Books: a Division of Penguin Books Ltd
Harmondsworth, Middlesex, England
Penguin Books Australia Ltd, Ringwood,
Victoria, Australia

First published in the U.S.A. 1969
Published in Great Britain by Macdonald 1970
Published in Puffin Books 1973
Copyright © Reader's Digest Books, Inc., 1969

Made and printed in Great Britain by
C. Nicholls & Company Ltd
Set in Linotype Pilgrim

Author's Note

Because there wasn't a great deal of news around, stories were once told in a nice garrulous fashion. These stories were not printed, of course, but were spoken, and the listeners wanted to know full details of each character who was introduced. The storyteller didn't say, 'Cor, son of Art, then entered the Great Hall with his hounds.' He said, 'Cor, son of Art, he whose mother came under the curse of the Grey Stones of the Bog of Julgill (that place well known as the abode of serpents of whom, Dringath, most horrible of all, swallowed Grometh of the Silver Hand and ten of his men) then entered the hall with five of his hounds, of whom he had received three from the Southern Geats for certain service of which I will tell later.'

That, to my mind, was a very much better way of telling a story and lasted for well over a thousand years and indeed is still in use in Ireland and other civilized nations.

However, in recent years the dictum was laid down that all details related in a story must pertain to the plot, and all action must be tied into the main action and everything must be tidy.

For myself, I reject these restrictions, and in telling the story which follows, I have returned to the older style. It is for me the proper style and more true to life. For all in life does not tie into a tidy tale, life being incomplete on this earth. What seem to us untidy ends here are neatly knotted, I assure you, in eternity.

Chapter 1

It was none other than Eric the Lame who first saw *Black Raven*, the warship of Harald the Hammer, returning home. It came from the south, across the crinkling sea and at no good pace, the wind being light and the oars poorly manned.

The Lame One saw it from the head of that cliff which is known as the Heroes' Leap to mark that place where the men of the West Vikings had jumped down upon the ships of the invading Geats in days gone by. He was ploughing the field on the cliff top, with the gulls swirling around him, crying in their fashion and searching for worms with glittering eyes. The lame man stopped his oxen and plough at the edge of the cliff and looked to seaward and marked to the south a dot no bigger than a fly on the empty space of the ocean.

A long time he watched it appear and disappear between the silver veils of mist that floated over the surface of the sea. Certainly when he first saw the ship he pondered whose it could be, for Harald the Hammer had long gone to the Southern Seas and was believed dead with all who had accompanied him on that journey.

He knew it was no ship of an enemy, for the Lord Sigurd was at peace with all, including even the Finns who delight both in war and sorcery. Also no raiding longship would come in broad daylight and with her oars but half-manned. Nor was this the season for raiding, for it was early spring and granaries would be empty and so no booty could be obtained by raiding.

But at last this ship came close enough for Eric the Lame to see the emblem of the Raven on its sail, and the colour of the sail itself, which was striped in red and white. And then he knew that this was the ship of Harald the Hammer, and leaving oxen and plough, ran immediately to inform the Lord Sigurd in his Great Hall, which stood in the centre of the Town of Ostmond on the north shore of the fjord of the same name.

He went in haste, scattering the geese which nibbled with hungry beaks at the fresh grass by the roadside before the Great Hall, and ran up the wooden stairs before the Hall where the doorkeeper demanded to know what was his business.

'Harald the Hammer returns,' cried the Lame One, and the doorkeeper, with a wild look of surprise, let him enter the Hall where Lord Sigurd was at meat with his lady and some of his war companions. Here his news was quickly given and a great silence fell on those in the Hall, for it seemed that Harald the Hammer, if he returned at all, must be returning from Valhalla, for all men long believed him dead.

But Sigurd commanded two ships to be sent out to meet him, the one commanded by Knute, his own son, and the other by Swen of Wodestrund, who was also called Swen the Red because of his hair and his beard. A great warrior he was, always to be found in the forefront of any fray, but it was known that he would die of a spear thrust from a dwarf. This fate had been revealed to him by one of those hags who live beside rivers spinning threads which record the fate of warriors. For this reason Swen of Wodestrund had a fear of all who were undersized.

With the ship of Knute went Eric the Lame, thus rewarded for being the first to bring the news of the return of Harald the Hammer, whom Lord Sigurd loved. Horsemen were also sent to summon others to a great feast which would be held to welcome Harald the Hammer home. These went to the Vikings of Skallgard and of Gurthwick, Yssfax and Holmfest beyond the mountains. And these same Vikings were asked to send messengers to the Swedes and Geats and Finns and Danes so that all would know of the return of Harald the Hammer and none be slighted at the thought that they had not been summoned to welcome him. In this way did Lord Sigurd keep peace among his neighbours.

'Tell Harald the Hammer,' said Lord Sigurd to his son Knute, 'that in all the lands he has been, he will find no greater welcome than that which waits him now in his homeland. Tell him I have aged one year for every month he has been away. And let this lame man be my cupbearer to him, for he is deserving of this honour, having been the first to bring such joyful news.'

This office greatly pleased Eric the Lame, who because of that injury inflicted on his leg at birth had never been able to follow the life of a warrior but had rather been condemned to the plough and other unmanly work.

Rejoicing then, he set off in the longship commanded by Knute, son of Sigurd, to welcome home *Black Raven*, the dark war vessel of Harald the Hammer.

Chapter 2

The cliff known as Heroes' Leap was soon thick with people watching the approach of *Black Raven*, which crawled northward towards the fjord slowly and purposefully like some sea beast which had been wounded and sought its cave for refuge. It was now possible from the head of the cliff to count the number of oars in use. There were but six to a side, less than half the normal number, and these were not plied with a good rhythm but raggedly, as if some who handled the oars did so with the last of their strength. The sail, now better seen, was much patched and stretched, and the emblem of the Raven upon it was no fine piece of embroidery, but an ugly daub, halfway between flying bird and flying dragon.

Those on the cliff watched silently, saying not a word about who might be alive and who dead of the men who followed Harald the Hammer to the Southern Seas seven years ago. One thing they knew, but still did not speak of – the tall figure at the steering oar, clad in a strange armour, was not Harald the Hammer. Nor did he seem to be anyone from the settlement.

A flock of sea birds was seen swirling below the edge of the cliff, crying as if in grief and making a great fluttering with their wings. The people turned from watching the ship to watching the gulls lest an omen be revealed to them. The gulls continued with their confused circling and crying and then slid away to the north around the headland. None was sure what was the meaning of this behaviour among the gulls, but they feared that it signified no good thing.

The two vessels which set out to meet that of Harald the Hammer were *Osprey* and *Sea Eagle*. *Osprey* was under the command of Knute, son of Sigurd, and it was on this vessel that Eric the Lame went with the drinking horn and the small butt of mead to pour the libation of welcome for Harald the Hammer. *Sea Eagle* was commanded by Swen of Wodestrund. As soon as these two captains had boarded their vessels, the rowers thrust them off from the stony beach of the fjord, half of them in the ships and half of them overboard to push them into deep water. They encouraged each other with shouts and laughter to be the first to float their vessels and the first to reach *Black Raven*, still out of sight behind the frowning walls of the fjord.

The water, it being yet winter, was cold as steel in the wind, but the men paid no attention to this, struggling waist-deep to launch the boats. And when at last they had thrust them out into the deep, they climbed aboard on the same oars with which, by swinging vigorously, they warmed themselves a few seconds later.

Away darted the two longships, *Osprey* and *Sea Eagle*, the quiet water gurgling against their bows and leaving behind a twisting, swirling wake of silver. They sped past the cliffs that guarded the entrance to the fjord and a mile beyond came upon *Black Raven* and, turning, glided to her, one on each side.

Knute, son of Sigurd, was first aboard *Black Raven*, stepping from the oars of his own men to those of Harald the Hammer's ship and so onto the thwarts on which her oarsmen sat. He glanced at the strange figure at the steering oar and then quickly about at the gaunt men manning the oars – men whose eyes seemed to be receding into their skulls.

'Where is your captain?' he cried. 'Speak quickly and speak true. Is not this the ship of Harald the Hammer?'

For answer the stranger pointed to the prow of the vessel and said. 'I have brought your captain home, for so he made me promise that I would do. But I fear I am too late and he is beyond the aid of any man on earth. Yet, God willing, he may last long enough to see again his own countryside and the Great Hall of his lord, Sigurd.'

Quickly Knute turned and sped along the rowing benches forward to where the sea dragon raised his head above the water on its neck of scales to form the bow of the ship. Here stores were kept for the voyage (as well as beneath the seats along the keel) and there was ample space for a bed. In this space, lying on a couch made of a few miserable skins, lay the wasted frame of Harald the Hammer. He was dressed in his corselet of ringed armour and his horned helmet lay beneath his head as a pillow. By his side, tarnished and rusted in many places, was his sword. His heavy round shield with its central boss of iron was propped against the side of the ship.

'What sickness has overtaken you to have brought you so low?' asked Knute, putting his hand on the face of Harald, only to find it as hot as a hearthstone.

'Is the Great Hall of Sigurd yet in sight?' asked Harald.

'No,' said Knute. 'But in a hundred strokes we will be within the fjord and in sight of the hall.'

'Then must I find the strength to live for one hundred strokes more,' said the other. 'Only if I can once again see the hall of my liege lord is there any hope for me.'

Knute leaped to his feet and shouted to those on *Osprey* and *Sea Eagle* to take the oars. Immediately so many men from *Osprey* and *Sea Eagle* boarded the vessel that she was in danger of sinking. They took the oars from the wrecks of men who had wielded them so feebly and made the water swirl with the lustiness of their strokes.

The ageing vessel at last came to life. From her weed-hung sides the water flew away in arrows of light. Quickly *Black Raven* picked up speed while the stranger at the helm used all his seaman's cunning to bring her into the mouth of the fjord. A white wave rose at her bow and spread outward past her as she thrust through the water. At last she entered the fjord and Swen of Wodestrund, who had come aboard, picked up Harald the Hammer in his huge arms, and holding him aloft, cried, 'See. There is the Great Hall of your Lord Sigurd, who himself waits to welcome you.'

But all this effort was in vain. For Harald the Hammer had closed his eyes in death, so weak that he could not even utter his death cry to summon the Valkyries to carry him on their wild horses beyond the clouds to Valhalla.

When he felt that Harald was dead, Swen put him gently again into the bottom of the ship and threw his cloak over him. Turning away he saw Eric the Lame standing by with the drinking horn and the vessel of mead. 'It was an omen indeed,' he said, 'that the Lord Sigurd sent a broken man to welcome Harald the Hammer home.'

Chapter 3

There was then no great celebration at Ostmond to welcome home the hero, Harald the Hammer. The chieftains summoned for that event arrived for his funeral, which was conducted in a style to suit a king because of the great love Sigurd had for the dead warrior.

First the body, having been washed and then anointed with sweet oil, was dressed in the best clothes and armour available. The cheeks were reddened with certain dyes prepared by the women, and the hair, which showed some streaks of grey, was also dyed and plaited in the proper fashion. The eyes were closed and silver coins placed over them to be instantly available to make whatever payment was required in another life. The nose and ears were stopped with cloths to prevent the entry of mischievous spirits into the body during the temporary absence of the soul. The great shield of Harald, refurbished but not made perfect (for it must show the blows of club and sword which it had sustained) was put at the warrior's side and his big war hammer placed in his hand. Two hunting dogs were killed and their bodies placed beside that of Harald. The body, thus arrayed, was laid upon a bed of pine boughs in the Great Hall of Lord Sigurd and the Death Feast was then given — a feast properly attended by all those chieftains previously sent for to welcome Harald home.

At this feast his praises were sung by all who knew him, each, to the accompaniment of the chords of Aldric the Harpist, composing some lines telling of an incident in the life of the warrior both to please him with praises – though dead – and excite the admiration of the gods who were known to be listening.

Rethel the Dane, long a companion of Harald, won great acclaim for his composition on the life of Harald, which ended with these lines :

> Gone is he from the small earth; plaything of the gods.
> No sword could hew his tree of life,
> Nor war hammer batter down his shield.
> Nor could foul age line his face with her cobwebs
> But some spell beyond the skill of men
> (Perhaps of the gods or of some others)
> Death – trapped him.
> He, whose battle-rage shook mountains
> Died silent as a fly. Perhaps, enchanted.

At the conclusion of these lines Rethel the Dane looked slyly at the stranger, whose name was Eusebius and who had brought back the *Black Raven* to Ostmond. He was present at the Death Feast, seated to the right of Sigurd as a guest of quality and the last noble companion of the dead warrior, the rest of the men who had returned being of base blood. The look Rethel the Dane gave Eusebius was not lost on the company, but the mead had not flowed in sufficient quantity for any to speak against the stranger, which would indeed violate the hospitality of the Great Hall.

Nonetheless, the Lord Sigurd frowned at the words and the look, though compelled to award a golden armband to the Dane for his death poem. Others followed with their tributes, though there were none who could speak of the recent adventures of the dead man, for all that survived of his crew were too stricken to attend the event. Of those who did speak, some, following the lead of the Dane, were bold enough to make some hint of enchantment or spell or black craft which had resulted in the death of Harald the Hammer, and when the horns of mead had circled the table several times Swen of Wodestrund raised his goblet to the stranger, and silence falling over the hall, said these words to him.

'It is plain to me, Eusebius, who comes from a land far distant from here, or so I have been told, that your gods have you under a special care. For of all the men who returned with you on that ship, *Black Raven*, which I now begin to believe to have been a vessel accursed, you alone are well enough to attend the Death Feast of Harald the Hammer. Though I do not wish you the slightest ill, you will forgive me being surprised at this, for you are in all a different mould of man from your captain and indeed from his other companions, all of whom could certainly claim to be as sturdily built.

'It is not in the slightest degree with the wish that you should share their misfortune that I ask you to explain how it is that you have managed to avoid it.'

This question was put against the wish of the Lord Sigurd, who had not himself had an opportunity of closely questioning the stranger, Eusebius, about the sickness of Harald the Hammer. The preparations for the funeral and the task of seeing that all those coming from afar to Ostmond were properly greeted and houses provided for them had occupied all his time. He would have preferred the whole matter to have been delayed until the funeral was over. Yet, Swen of Wodestrund having raised the matter, a reply could not be refused without suspicion – already aroused – running high against the stranger.

Eusebius then, who had drunk only as much of the mead as courtesy demanded, rose to answer Swen, and such a silence fell upon the hall that only the hiss and crackle of the great logs in the fire could be heard.

'You do me great honour and a great kindness, Swen of Wodestrund,' said Eusebius, 'to thus question me before this mighty assemblage of fighting men of your country – kings, chiefs, and warriors whose deeds are known even in such countries as they themselves have never visited. For you give me now an opportunity to answer, at one time, the questions which I know gnaw at the minds of all; that same question which you have put to me so openly and in such fair words – namely, why others should sicken on *Black Raven* but I should be in good health; why indeed Harald the Hammer who was my friend should die, while I, of smaller build, as you say, and therefore of less strength (as you suppose) should live.

'First then I will tell you, without boasting, something of myself and of the country from which I come, and for the truth of what I say you can, in time, turn to those of the *Black Raven*'s crew who now live among you and have been returned to their country by no other skill but my own.'

At this there was a rumbling of anger, for the men of the fjord believed themselves more skilled in sea usage than any other people in any part of the world.

'I see that my words do not entirely agree with your mood,' said Eusebius, 'and yet I must in all honesty insist that were it not for my skill, not one of the men of this fjord would have been able to return here. For you are accustomed, no doubt, to making long voyages by sea, yet always within reach of land and in this way you go about the world. But my skill is such that I can travel over the waters of the ocean, on which there are not signs to say at what place I may be, and yet by carefully examining the sky I can bring a ship safely to its port. And you will learn by questioning the others that when the *Black Raven* had passed through that gateway which gives entrance to the Southern Sea and out into the ocean, she was driven ten days before gales to the west and at that time was even by the reckoning of Harald the Hammer three hundred leagues from the nearest land.

'Which of you here, then, in such circumstances, could have come safely to this place, there being no signposts on the ocean to guide you? Does such a feat lie within your skill? Do I hear any man among you say that he could do this thing?'

But none in the Great Hall made any answer.

'Let us put aside these vain boastings then,' said Eusebius, 'and let me say plainly who I am and from where I come and then answer your question concerning my health and the sickness of all others aboard the *Black Raven*.

'As for who I am, that is soon told. I am Eusebius of Tyre, a great city in the land of Phoenicia, hard by the sea at the eastern end of the Southern Ocean. In that city I am a man of no small wealth and have at my command a fleet of ten ships which carry goods to many parts of the world – from the Western Isles, of which you may perhaps have heard, to the southernmost portions of the Land of Punt, where there are many marvels; among them a race of men who, fullgrown, are no bigger than boys of ten, and who blow a certain dart from a tube which will kill the greatest warrior in less than three breaths.

'It was at sea that I met Harald the Hammer, he being in *Black Raven* and I being captain of my own galley whose name in your tongue is *Swan of Light*. My galley was at that time returning from the land of Egypt with a cargo of corn and the oil of a certain tree, also rare wood which is perfumed like flowers, also the feathers of a bird that stands as high as a man and can run faster than a horse. This bird is called ostrich, but the name will of course have no significance for you at all.'

'It will scarcely be bigger than our golden eagle,' said Rethel the Dane.

'If you refer to the mountain eagle, then the relationship is as follows,' said Eusebius smoothly. 'As the mountain eagle is to the sparrow so is the ostrich to the mountain eagle. However,' he added, 'the ostrich cannot fly. But it is not to discuss birds that I stand now before you.

'You will have no difficulty in believing that *Black Raven*, having sighted my galley and knowing that she was richly laden coming from the land of Egypt, gave chase to seize her, for as I collect my treasures by trading with others, exchanging goods by barter, so I know that such dealing is reckoned by you to be shameful, and fortune is to be won by war alone. I will not detail that chase which lasted through a day and a night and into the following day. Suffice it to say that in the end the men of *Black Raven* proved more hardy than my own rowers and the long ship drew closer and was soon in position to board.

'Harald the Hammer stood first among the boarders and commanded his men to lay their oars out level and lock them so that he could run along them and jump into the galley. So fine a man clad in chain mail, helmeted with the ox horns and wielding his great hammer of war, seemed to me like a god, and I decided, seeing him standing so splendid in the sun, to spare his life.'

No rule of hospitality could stop the roar of outrage that came from the guests at the audacity of the stranger in saying that the life of Harald the Hammer, armed for war, had lain in his hands. Men leapt for sword and buckler to avenge the hero whose body, stiff in death and wasted by illness, lay in the middle of the Great Hall, on its bed of pine boughs. But the Lord Sigurd, with a mighty shout, reduced them to silence and himself scarcely able to contain his anger, although the host, asked Eusebius to quickly explain what he meant by such a boast.

For answer Eusebius opened a small case of wood which he had by his side, and which had passed unknown up to this point, and from it took a weapon consisting of a length of polished bone with a piece of animal gut stretched taut between the two ends. To this strange contraption he fitted a more slender stick barbed at one end like a spear and feathered at the other. Then turning to Lord Sigurd he said, 'If you are willing that I use this weapon, I will show how I had the life of Harald the Hammer at that time in my hands.'

'Do what you will,' said Lord Sigurd. 'None shall harm you.'

'I see upon the wall there a buckler of great size,' said Eusebius. 'Has such a buckler ever been pierced by sword or spear?'

The question seemed so foolish to the company that all laughed, which Eusebius took as indicating that no sword or spear could ever penetrate such a shield.

'If I place this missile through that buckler,' said the Phoenician, 'will you then grant that this same missile could have pierced the shirt of ring mail with which Harald the Hammer was clad and so killed him?'

'That I will grant and readily,' said Sigurd.

'See then how his life was in my hands to save or take,' said Eusebius, and bending the bow, released the arrow. It fled so swiftly across the Great Hall that none saw it pass though they heard the hiss of its flight. But all heard the thwack it dealt the buckler and all saw the arrow buried to the feathers in the giant shield, enough penetrating the other side to pin a man's heart to his backbone.

'So I saved the life of Harald the Hammer,' said

Eusebius. 'For I told my bowmen not to use their weapons, but instead to bring out the nets and make them prisoners.'

'You use nets in wars?' asked Sigurd.

'That is true,' said the Phoenician.

'But it is shameful!' cried Swen of Wodestrund.

The Phoenician shrugged. 'Tell me, Swen of Wodestrund,' he said, 'which is the greater shame – to win or to lose? To be victor or be vanquished?'

'To be vanquished,' replied the other.

'And so I won,' said the Phoenician, 'with the nets. For I had soon entangled with them all the men of *Black Raven* who were not cut down by my spearmen and made them captive.

'Of those whom I brought back on the *Black Raven*, all were my captives – including he who lies now dead on his bier amongst us. And I set all free. Tell me, do you think I would set men free only to cause them to sicken and die later?'

To this not even Swen of Wodestrund dared to make a reply.

Chapter 4

'I did not, though that power lay in my hands, use my captives with dishonour nor put them, when they had returned with me to Tyre, to work which is suitable to oxen but repugnant to men, and particularly to warriors,' continued Eusebius. 'I required only of them that they give their word not to lift their hand against me or my people or attempt to escape. He who lies dead there acted most bravely. You have heard his companions with approval make verses concerning his life amongst you. I would myself make a verse concerning his life in my country of Phoenicia. If it should not match that of Rethel the Dane, yet I beg your generosity in receiving it, for I make now a verse in a language which is not my own and my tongue may then prove but the clumsy servant of my mind.'

The Phoenician glanced then at Aldric the Harpist, who plucked from his instrument the notes needed to introduce a poet, and Eusebius told in verse how Harald the Hammer had been received as a chief in the country of Phoenicia and had taken part in many onslaughts by sea and by land against the enemies of the Phoenicians, and had been held in the highest honour among them. The verses concluded with the lines:

> Hear how, striving between that night and day
> Which men call death and life, he yet made play
> Of life and death and mid his teeming foes
> Bid one take to his bed: another stay.

> So gift of death or gift of further light
> He gave; nor feared himself descent into the night
> Until the Dark Angel, silent as the dew
> Bade him follow her in dreadful flight.

This style of making poetry was so strange that none in the Great Hall applauded when the Phoenician had finished, but looked puzzled one at the other, that words should be put at the ends of lines that had similar sounds though different meanings – which was never done anywhere to their knowledge. But Aldric the Harpist looked at Eusebius with admiration and cried, 'A drink for he who gives new music to old words. No man before in my time has shown such word craft. If the stranger makes swordplay as aptly as he makes wordplay, then he was indeed a fit companion to Harald the Hammer.'

Now Aldric was not only harpist but warrior, and held in high regard by all. So when he had made his tribute to Eusebius, the others agreed with him and smote the table with their hands and fists to make an uproar over such word skill. Sigurd, unfastening from his own neck a necklace worked in massive gold and set about with stones of blue, red, and green, gave it to the Phoenician to honour his poem.

'You teach us many things that are new, Phoenician,' he said. 'Strange use of weapons, strange use of words. For that same tool which you used to send a dart through the great shield upon my wall, we use, in another way – to make fire.'

'That I know,' said Eusebius. 'But had none thought to put the bow to the use of war?'

'No,' said Sigurd. 'And for this reason: amongst us it is regarded as lacking in manliness to kill an opponent from some distance off. Do not, I beg you, think that in this I hold you or your people coward. There are different usages among different peoples, and only a fool blames the bear for not fighting like the wolf. Yet for us it is no honour to kill or be killed except within the sword reach of our enemy – grappling thigh to thigh and arm to arm.'

'You speak truly, Lord Sigurd,' said Swen. 'Although I will not violate your rules of hospitality by making any criticism of our noble guest, yet none of us can claim to have heard from him of any deed of arms worthy of notice. For to trap fighting men in nets is not to be reckoned valorous, nor is to kill from afar an action worthy of praise among warriors or gods.'

'I seek not the praise of warrior or gods,' said Eusebius. 'These things are trifles in my opinion, and worth only the strivings of children. If there should be among you those who doubt my courage, do not look to me to set your doubts at rest. I care nothing for them. I am not come here to prove myself the hero of Tyre, nor to lose my life to gain the acclaim of a hall filled with warriors. That is no prize which I would value. What I have come here for is far beyond that in worth – but I will not speak of it at this time.

'I have told you how I captured Harald the Hammer and his ship and his companions, how they were brought back to Tyre, how they became allies of mine for five years in wars against my enemies. And I now say that at the end of this five years I gave them leave to return, laden with gifts and the spoils of war, and asked only that I be myself allowed to accompany them in their journey to their homeland. This request I made because of that particular prize which I myself seek and which is to be found, I learned, in this part of the world.

'The rest is soon told. When we passed through those gates that guard the entrance to the Southern Seas we were driven three hundred leagues to the west by a white gale.

To lighten the vessel all the spoils of war and the rich trophies and prizes won by Harald and his companions were thrown overboard. More than half of the ship's company were lost in this gale which raged for ten days. Waves higher than those cliffs which tower over your harbour boarded us and swept the longship from end to end, carrying away with them many of our comrades whose cries even were lost in the fury of the wind and the raging of the waters. Each man then saved his own life and when the water and wind abated, there were left aboard but fifteen men, including Harald the Hammer and myself. The other ships that set out with us were lost.

'Then it was found that all food was gone and but two skins of water remained – sufficient for the number of men we had for eight days at best.

'I counselled that this water be given out only in a small amount each day and at nighttime when, the heat of the sun being gone, it would longest remain in the bodies of those who received it and do the most good. I might as well have advised wolves to caution as Harald and his men. They would accept no such advice, but drank their fill, relying as they said upon Odin to send more rain from the skies – which Odin failed to do.

'So all was gone in two days that might, with care, have lasted eight. Since my counsel did not prevail, I asked that my part of the water be put aside in a jar which had remained aboard unbroken. I did not desire to rely on the generosity of the gods without first making some provision for my own safety. This was agreed. When the others had no water, I yet had some. They drank from the sea. I drank sparingly of my supply. I remained well. They sickened and some died.'

'You did not think to share your water with your companions?' asked Rethel the Dane.

'So I did,' said Eusebius, 'but only with those who had not drunk of sea water. With these I shared my supply, but such men as Harald's cannot contain their appetites. All within a few days had drunk of the cool and lovely ocean – some small amounts, some copiously. Those who drank sparingly became sick. Those who drank more heavily died – among them Harald the Hammer. I alone drank only fresh water and had strength enough to bring the vessel home. I will not speak of skill, which I have already mentioned and which I say, without boasting, I possess in greater degree than any man who has sailed from this fjord.

'This then is my tale which you have asked of me at an improper time, for we are here to give the last feast to Harald the Hammer. Of the matter which brought me here, I will perhaps speak at another time.'

The Phoenician then seated himself, and Edessa, wife of Lord Sigurd, herself brought to him a horn of mead and set before him plenty of meat and bread, for she had liked his verses and also it was right that she should so honour him.

When the feast was done, and the moon (tilted like a stricken ship) had risen over the mountains which lay behind the town, torches were called for in the greatest quantity and the body of Harald the Hammer was laid upon a bier to be taken to the burial ship – itself none other than *Black Raven*, newly fitted for its last sad voyage. Those who now rose to carry the bier of Harald to the ship were Swen of Wodestrund, Rethel the Dane, Hjalmar of Holmfest, Eric of the Skallgard Vikings, and Knute, son of Sigurd. The warriors present reached for their shields and swords, and walking before and behind the bier as it was taken solemnly from the Great Hall, beat upon their bucklers so that the steel rang in the night like the sound of battle to awaken the gods to the coming of Harald the Hammer.

A hundred torches lighted the way to the ship, itself laden richly with meat, wine, mead, weapons of war, and also trophies of the chase. The bier was placed across the central thwarts and a torch put in each of the tholes which held the oars. The sail was set – that same sail of the *Black Raven* which the vessel had carried on its journey home – and then the ship, ringed in the light of torches, was towed out of the fjord. The sail, catching a light wind from the east, filled, and the ship, ringed in fire, swiftly gathered speed and slipped in the moonlight towards the Island of the Dead beyond the western horizon.

And in the Great Hall of Sigurd, Eusebius the Phoenician sat alone, deep in thought and watched, with questioning eyes, by Eric the Lame, who had remained to wait on him.

Chapter 5

Harald the Hammer having been sent upon his last voyage, the chiefs who had come to Ostmond remained awhile with their men as guests of Lord Sigurd, who delighted in feasting them and loading them with presents – rings, armbands, helmets, swords, corselets of mail, and bucklers with great bosses of iron cunningly overlaid either with silver or gold wire twisted into strange designs. Since he was a great lord, he had a vast store of these things taken in campaigns which he had waged in his youth from places deep into the mountain hinterlands of the land of the Swedes to the rivers and marshes and forests of those lands across the water and to the south, which were called the Gothlands. The plains of the Geats had many times, in his youth, heard the ring of his sword and the shrilling of his war horn, as had also the miserable forests and bogs of the Finns and the lone valleys of the Franks, clad with pleasant grasses sweet in summer with bird song.

It was a delight then to him to host a multitude of men, to provide for them food in plenty, and great fires to be warmed by, and shelter, and when some wished to go (having before them a long sea journey) he yet begged them to stay. If they refused, he filled their ships with food and gifts of many kinds, for there was never among the sea lords a chieftain with a greater heart or stronger sword arm than Sigurd of the West Vikings.

When Sigurd then had been given every opportunity to amply demonstrate his hospitality, and those who remained were determined to depart, he proposed in the Great Hall that on the following day those who remained hunt wolf in the mountain valleys to the north and east.

'My herdsmen tell me there are large packs of wolves ranging the lower mountains with frost-stiff pelts, their breath-cloud thick about them,' he said. 'How many, Hjalmar of Holmfest, think you we shall bring back dead to the Great Hall tomorrow night?'

'I have a hundred men to my back,' said Hjalmar of Holmfest. 'I shall not think well of our day's work unless we have accounted for ten wolves among us.'

'And you, Eric of Skallgard?'

'If they are as numerous as you have said, I say six shall fall to the axe and six to the spear,' said Eric. So each chief in the Great Hall made his boast and the total was that there would be killed over fifty wolves – a thing which had not been done since the time of Lettfin, father to Sigurd, when there had been a great gathering of Vikings and they had hunted wolves for sport before descending on the Danes. Of Danes there had been killed in the battle that followed only twenty-five, so hardy the Danes proved in battle. And so arose that saying that one Dane was worth two wolves, which was believed ever afterwards, and it became the custom of the Danes to wear the skin of a wolf over their armour with the head, teeth bared, upon the helmet. The men of Sigurd wore, however, the skin of the bear, which they thought a more worthy creature.

Now Sigurd had proposed the wolf hunt in part to provide sport for his guests, but also to give an outlet for angry feelings which were beginning to arise amongst them and were directed some against the Phoenician and some, such is the nature of men, against those who wished ill to the same Phoenician. It had become plain to him that the vast assemblage of men who feasted daily in his

Great Hall, having nothing to occupy themselves other than eating, drinking, and wrestling, were dividing over the stranger.

One group, led by Swen of Wodestrund, harboured ill feelings against him, and said that while it might be indeed true that he had not himself been directly the cause of the death of Harald the Hammer, nonetheless he was certainly versed in witchcraft. It was plain, said these, that that storm which had driven the *Black Raven* into the Western Ocean for three hundred leagues had risen at the bidding of the stranger who well knew, using the storm, how to get all aboard the ship into his powers.

How else, they asked, could he have brought the ship back safely and how else could he have so well preserved his own health, when others, much stronger, had died and become gravely ill? Not without reason have the bards of the Vikings warned that the idle hand is more dangerous than the one that wields the war hammer, and the idle tongue a greater destroyer of men than poisoned meat.

Against this group were others led by Herebeald, a king among the Geats, from the lands south of the Dane lands, who said that all on *Black Raven* owed their lives to the stranger who had brought the ship back home, and should then place themselves entirely at his service, their kinfolk as well. This was a smaller party, however, for few think highly of the reasoning of a Geat, though at swordplay they were held men to be reckoned with. Indeed, great swords were made in olden times by the smiths of the Geats – among them the Singer, which was the blade borne by Sigurd and Lettfin before him, and also the sword Icefire of Rethel the Dane, which his grandfather had won from Alric, King of the Geats in those times.

So, his guests being divided into two camps and idle,

the wolf hunt was arranged, and Eusebius, the Phoenician, was also invited to take part, though it was tactfully requested of him that he should not use that weapon whose power he had demonstrated in the Great Hall.

'Spear, axe, blade, or hammer are yours to choose among, however,' said Sigurd. 'And be assured that your wants will be nobly supplied when you have made your choice.'

'I will take blade then,' said Eusebius. 'But let it be light and of little size.'

Such a request was by no means easy to fill, for the notable blades in the armoury of Sigurd were all of great size, it being the custom to match blade to man in this proportion: that a man's sword should, put upright before him, reach to the level of his chest. But the Phoenician took a sword fashioned for boys, though of splendid metal, and called Wasp. From that time he was named by some, Small Sword, and men laughed at him and said that he intended to carry to the wolf hunt only a stick for scratching fleas and would certainly be found not among the warriors but among the servingmen at the camp where the food for the hunters would be prepared.

He also took with him, as cupbearer and attendant, not one of the fighting men who followed the other chiefs, but Eric the Lame, who had never yet been to war and, being a broken man, could not be expected to fight or bear any worthy part in the coming hunt.

Though others mocked at this, the Lord Sigurd, however, commended the Phoenician on this choice and said to him he would find Eric the Lame staunch though unable to move with speed. 'His mother, while carrying him, was compelled to make a journey to the settlement of Issfirth with several others,' he said. 'Because it was near her time she could not travel fast, and toward evening of the second day, when her party had entered a certain forest, cried out that her time had come.

'A camp was made and in a while, after the setting of the sun, she was delivered of her son. But it chanced that at that moment, the midwife, turning at her work, beheld a troll standing outside the circle of the fire, ready to snatch the child. She shrieked at it and threw a brand in its direction and so drove that evil thing away. But the gaze of the troll had fallen upon the leg of the baby and so the leg never quickened rightly (it being the foul power of trolls that they turn to stone that which lives), and so the boy was born lame. Yet he is of a good line of men, for his father bore himself well in our wars against the Danes, and his mother (now dead) did not fear to clout any who ventured a rude jest at her expense or that of her son.

'This also is true about him, that being less active than others in matters of sport and war, he has had time to think more deeply. But he gives only wintry counsels. Spring never yet came to his heart or mind.'

Herebeald, King of the Geats, however, was concerned that Eusebius had chosen Eric the Lame as his servant. 'We cannot delay or lag behind the others for that broken man,' he said. 'Leave him and come with us and get your full share of the sport.'

But Eusebius said he would still keep the lame man for his bearer. So it fell out that when the hunters started for the mountain valleys in which lay the lairs of the wolves, though all went off together from the camp, the Phoenician and his guide were soon left behind. The mass of the hunters had gained the foothills of the mountain, which raised their glittering snow-clad flanks in a wall to the east and north, while Eusebius still struggled across the flatlands where rags of last summer's growth broke here and there the bitter coat of snow. Eric the Lame led a small pony on which to bring back their quarry and carried a spear while Eusebius went some distance ahead with two wolfhounds generously loaned to him by Sigurd.

They came at length to the foothills, and entering a fold between two rock-girt hills, found the snow drifted deep within. Then Eric took from the pony the special shoes of gut on which the Vikings were accustomed to walk over deep snow, and binding a pair to the feet of the stranger instructed him how he was to walk with them.

'My Lord,' said Eric, 'is it indeed your wish to meet with wolves this day?'

'That is so,' said the other. 'For though I have heard much of the creatures and have seen skins and heads, yet I have never seen one alive.'

'Then I can take you to the place where lives the great wolf in these parts who is known to all men as Torfka. His eyes, it is said, are of red fire and his size the same as the baggage pony. It is said also that all the other wolves hunt for him, and bring him sheep and deer, goats and the limbs of cattle. But he is so fearful that they will not live with him, but only serve him. He is the king of all the wolves. If you kill him, you will win much credit amongst the others.'

'Who would wish to kill so magnificent a beast?' said Eusebius.

'You do well, my lord, to avoid him,' said Eric with a secret smile.

'I did not say that I wished to avoid him. Only that I did not wish to kill him,' replied the Phoenician. 'If you know where he is likely to be found, then take me there that I may see him.'

They went on their snowshoes up the first valley, which was small, and mounting a wall of rock at the end found beyond a deeper valley, clad with pine and larch, rocky and precipitous with, at its bottom, a raging torrent black with winter cold. This valley rose steeply up the side of a tremendous mountain mass before them. It was heavily forested about its base and so steep toward the peak that the dark rocks, like defending towers and parapets, thrust out against the sky, naked of snow, which could find no place to rest on them. Around this austere peak the winds hissed and screamed, and rags of cloud now hid and now revealed the gaunt summit. Between forest and peak was a vast field of stone, glaciated in parts and in others stripped bare by the wind. Eric halted and pointed to a sentinel rock that stood boldly out from this desolation of stone.

'There is the lair of Torfka,' he said. 'All know it but none visit it. In that lair lie the bones of sheep and shepherd, side by side.'

'Can you travel so great a distance?' asked Eusebius.

'I can, my lord,' said Eric. 'For my lame leg is but a bone and feels no pain, and my good leg is, as a result, twice as strong as any man's. Also I will make use of the four good legs of the pony.' He did not, however, mount the beast, which was laden with stores, but seized it by the tail and so was pulled along at a good speed behind. In this manner they had by noon passed through the forest area and were on the verge of that vast place of stones where Torfka made his lair.

Here they refreshed themselves with food, stopping but a little while, for the cold wind, laden with tiny splinters of ice, allowed them no comfort in resting. Then on again, and so reached halfway to the place where was the lair of the great wolf. The pony now began to tremble in every part and would go no farther, for she scented the wolf, but the hounds, catching the same scent, lifted their grey muzzles to the sky and bayed their deep challenge to Torfka to come out and battle with them, fang to fang. Held firm on their leashes, they thrust and struggled to scramble up toward the lair, and Eusebius praised them, saying that the hounds indeed had the courage of their master, Lord Sigurd.

'Let them slip!' cried Eric. 'It is plain from their baying that Torfka is in his den. They will keep him there until we arrive.' So the Phoenician freed the hounds from their leashes, and they flung themselves over the steep field of stones to the den of the great wolf.

The pony was now hobbled and left behind, for the poor beast would go no farther, and Eusebius and the Lame One followed the dogs and had soon come to the den also. Here the dogs howled and bayed but would not venture closer than a spear's throw to the mouth of the den, which lay at the base of that great stone they had seen from afar.

'Think you that the wolf is inside?' asked Eusebius.

'That is certainly the case,' said Eric. 'Stay close to the dogs, for he will be out in a minute.' He then took the spear, which was his only weapon, and awaited the appearance of the wolf.

But when, after some time, Torfka did not appear, though the dogs kept up their sharp barking and baying, the Phoenician, wrapping a cloak of fur about his arm for a shield, drew his sword and said that he would enter the cave and visit Torfka in his own lair. Nor could Eric dissuade him, for the Phoenician gave no heed to his warnings of the size and savagery of the wolf, but passing the dogs, went firmly to the mouth of the den and was soon lost in the darkness of the interior.

He was scarcely inside before there came a snarling and yelping from behind and Eric turned to see the great grey wolf hurling towards them.

The hounds turned and threw themselves on the foe, but, scarcely pausing, the great wolf ripped open the throat of one of the hounds with its jaws and lamed the other with one swift slash of its fangs.

Eric threw his spear, which missed the wolf – none other than Torfka himself – and then Torfka jumped through the entrance of the lair. Now came from the den the uproar of battle between man and wolf, which lasted for some time; then quiet fell so that Eric was sure that Eusebius had lost his life to the fangs of Torfka.

He waited a little while, thinking perhaps to see the wolf reappear, when he would try once more to kill him with his spear and so avenge his master. But no movement coming from the cave, he concluded that at that moment the wolf was eating his master with horrid relish. One hound was dead and the other in such bad state that it could not walk. Nor could Eric carry it, so he dispatched the hound with his spear and turned to go down the mountain again to the pony when he heard a shout from inside the cave and in a moment out came the Phoenician, with much blood on him but not, it seemed, gravely wounded.

'I thought you dead, my lord,' cried Eric. 'By what sorcery have you managed to kill the wolf?'

'Who captured Harald the Hammer and all his men with a net could scarcely fail to trap a wolf with a cloak,' replied Eusebius. 'I confess, however, that had I carried a bigger sword, I could not, in so small a space, have used it. Go get the pony, for the wolf is dead and I will make a garment of his skin.'

'Master,' said Eric, 'of all who set out to hunt wolf today, none dared come to this part lest they meet with he whose den you entered and whom you have slain. You have indeed reaped the honours of the hunt, though some will say it was by sorcery.'

Eric then begged Eusebius to suck clean any bite wounds he had received from the wolf, for it was often the case that men bitten by wolves became themselves of the same nature as wolves. But the Phoenician said that of all creatures on earth man was the most savage, and if then he became like a wolf, he would in this be made gentler. But he sucked his wounds, which were all on his hands and arms, nonetheless.

Chapter 6

The Phoenician stayed many weeks with Lord Sigurd after the rest of the host had departed each to his own country. When, however, all had gone and only the Phoenician remained, the Lord Sigurd summoned him privately to inquire into that hidden purpose which Eusebius had hinted lay behind his decision to come to the northlands.

Not wishing, however, to rudely question him about this out of time, he asked Eusebius whether there was any service he could render him of any sort. If so, he had but to name it and it would be gladly offered.

'Perhaps,' said Sigurd, 'you have a mind to travel farther in these parts either by the land or by the sea. If so, I will put at your disposal an armed band of trusty men to accompany you over the mountains or oceans.

'If it is by sea you wish to go (and I advise going by sea, for in the inland mountains of these parts are said to be many hazards, including tree creatures and water creatures against which no man can prevail), I will provide you with a ship and forty men of the most venturesome spirit to be found.'

'I am grateful indeed that you have thought fit to mention this matter,' said Eusebius, 'for it is indeed time for me to be about that business which brought me here in the first case. I had hoped that Harald the Hammer, when he had taken his ease in his own land, would accompany me on this journey ahead, for he was a hardy man and one I loved – though I do not speak readily of these things and

I know there are still men who put his death to my account.'

'It is shameful that this should be so,' said Sigurd.

'It would be strange if it were not,' said Eusebius. 'Among all men, those who are different are suspect. But I would talk of my quest, and since you are curious, I will lay all things plainly before you.

'You may recall that during the Death Feast of Harald I made some mention of that country I come from and of my standing there, which is that of merchant – a profession far different from yours, which is that of lord and warrior. Now in my own calling I have voyaged to many parts of the world, and you may recall that I said that I did not have to go to the Land of Punt to see marvels but could find them in the land to the south of mine, once inhabited by a powerful people, but now laid all to waste by an invasion of enemies.'

'I recall all of that well,' said Sigurd.

'Well then,' continued the Phoenician, 'these people who live to the south of my land and are called Israelites are deeply versed in magic, in sorcery, in witchcraft, and in all the arts dealing with those beings which, though invisible to men, are nonetheless known to surround us all. This knowledge has come to them from ancient times and they keep it jealously to themselves. With it they are able to perform very many wonders.'

'What sorts of wonders?' asked Sigurd.

'Wonders of every kind,' said Eusebius. 'I will relate a few of them. It happened that on one occasion the whole of this people was called upon to make a journey across a desert in which there was no water and no food to eat. All were starving. Their chief then struck upon a rock with a staff which he held and immediately there gushed from the rock a plentiful supply of cool water – sufficient to satisfy the thirst of all the people of that nation. Then, their thirst quenched, the skies clouded up, not with rain clouds, but with clouds of bread, and this bread fell from the sky and covered the ground and the people had all they wished to eat. Also this bread gave them greater strength than any of their own baking.

'Again these people were at one time enslaved and, escaping under this same chief, they came to a vast sea barring their path. The sea opened before them and they were able to pass across the bed of the ocean with the raging waters piled like walls on either side and fish flapping out their lives on the wet sands at their feet. When they had crossed, the enemy plunged after them, but the sea enveloped them and they were all drowned.'

'Why did they flee their enemies?' asked Sigurd.

'To escape,' said Eusebius.

'Why did they not fight?' asked Sigurd. 'It is surely better to die a brave man than to live a coward.'

'That view is not common to all men,' said the Phoenician softly.

'Was it by sorcery that the sea opened before them?' asked Sigurd.

'They prayed to their god and so the sea opened,' said the other.

'To which of their gods did they pray?'

'They have but one,' said Eusebius.

'One?' cried Sigurd in surprise.

'Only one,' repeated the other.

'This is something beyond belief,' said Sigurd. 'I do not see how they could be so foolish as to suppose that there is but one god, and that for this reason: it is very painful for a man to be alone, for a day or several days or for a week or even for a month. Now if that is so for a man and for so small a length of time, how can they suppose that a god could endure to be alone for not just a day or a week or a month but for all the days, weeks, and months that the earth has endured and will endure? Certainly he would want the company of other gods to drink wine with and hold feasts and to fight and hunt and have other sports.

'One god by himself would be in misery, and who would ever say that a god would choose to live in misery? So certainly there must be other gods and very many of them. Also how could one god look after all the things of earth that need the attention of gods? Is it reasonable to say that one god should have the direction of war, and the same god should have the direction of peace, which is the opposite of war? Is one god to have the direction of birth among women and goats and cattle and sheep, and that same god to have the direction of death also among women and goats and cattle and sheep?

'Certainly such a god would become very muddled and would find the task altogether beyond his ability. So again it follows that there must be many gods and any nation which says that there is but one god must indeed be a nation of fools. I can readily see how it is that they have been defeated in war and made slaves, as you say, and are entirely without courage, fleeing from their enemies instead of resisting them to death.'

Eusebius smiled. 'It is pointless to discuss these matters,' he said. 'I deal with the wonders which these people are capable of producing in their own favour. But perhaps you tire of stories of these wonders?'

'By no means,' said Sigurd. 'Tell me more of them.'

'Good,' replied the Phoenician. 'On one occasion, when they met in a great host to attack a certain city, which was well fortified by stout walls, they blew on their war trumpets and beat on their cymbals and the walls of that city fell to the ground and so they were able to take it with ease.

'Again on another occasion when they were hard-pressed in battle (for you are not to presume that they are not great warriors) their chief, standing with arms outstretched at the bidding of their god, caused the sun to hold still in the sky, and because of this they defeated their enemies.

'Also they had in their chief place (before it was destroyed) a certain pool around which all those who were sick gathered each day. A spirit called an angel smote this pool with a stick and troubled the water, and whoever of the sick first got into the pool after that was cured. Some of their great chiefs have lived for four or five hundred years, and one at least never died but was taken bodily up into their Valhalla, which they call Heaven. Indeed I could recite wonders which have occurred among them for many hours and you may say that there is nothing of which man can conceive in the nature of marvels that they have not been able to perform.'

'Certainly they are a strange people,' said Sigurd. 'But have they no heroes among them who, without sorcery, slew monsters of some kind? It is by feats of arms that I am moved more than tales of magic.'

'They have indeed such heroes,' said Eusebius. 'For one, though small and indeed only a boy, slew a giant so huge that no warrior dared withstand him. And one of their heroes slew in battle scores of his enemies, but being captured by treachery and blinded, pulled down the building in which he was kept prisoner with his bare hands and in his death slew more than when he was alive. Another killed a monster called a lion with nothing more than the jawbone of a small horse. They have heroes to match those of any nation.'

'We have not come yet to your own purpose in voyaging here,' said Sigurd.

'We come to it now,' replied Eusebius. 'For of all the wonders which these people are known to have performed there is one which interests me especially. And that is the bringing of a man back from the dead.'

'They are capable of such a thing?' asked Sigurd, his interest now more thoroughly awakened.

Eusebius gave a shrug. 'I cannot be sure,' he said. 'I have made inquiries. All my inquiries insist that it is so. And yet I cannot be certain. The story goes in this manner:

'One among them, deeply versed in their lore promised that he would raise himself from the dead. He had many enemies and made more by making such a promise. He was seized, accused of false swearing and other things, and put to death by being nailed to a wooden cross. Three days later, having been buried, it is said that he rose from the dead and lived on earth a further two months, being seen by many, before he went to the place you call Valhalla.'

'What is the rest of that story?' asked Sigurd, who still did not understand why the Phoenician should have come to the northlands.

'It is said that this man was able to raise himself from the dead as a result of drinking from a particular Cup which he had. He said that those who drank from that Cup, like he, would never die. I seek the Cup.'

'You seek the Cup here?' exclaimed Sigurd, astonished.

Eusebius shook his head. 'It was taken from the land called Judea in which this man died and brought by a friend to the White Island lying to the west of these lands, and I believe it to be still there.'

'I have never heard of this Cup,' said Sigurd. 'What was the name of the man who drank from it and raised himself from the dead?'

'Jesus,' said the Phoenician.

'I have not heard of him either,' said Sigurd. 'But if you wish to journey to the White Island, I will give you a ship and men and a pilot and you will be at liberty to go there and seek your Cup of Life.'

Eusebius remained silent for a while. Then he said gravely, 'Lord Sigurd, in my own land I have everything that can be desired. One thing only I fear. That is something common to all men – death. For this reason I seek the Cup of Eternal Life. I thank you heartily for your offer of a ship and men to take me to the White Island, where I believe that Cup is now to be found.'

Lord Sigurd looked at the Phoenician with curiosity. 'It is odd indeed that so brave a man as you should fear such a trifle. But a ship you shall have, as promised, and I hope it will help put an end to your fear.'

Chapter 7

A longship of eighty-five feet, seating forty rowers and
with room for all their gear and stores for a voyage of some
weeks, was now given to the Phoenician by Lord Sigurd.
The prow of this vessel, which had but lately wedded the
ocean, was carved in the likeness of the worm Snikhail
that guards a certain lake in the interior of the northlands
– a lake containing a vast treasure and surrounded by trees
so dense and tall that the sunlight never falls upon its surface. For this reason the lake is called the Dark Water.

'This ship is most suited to your purpose,' Sigurd said,
'for you seek, I think, a treasure in the deep Lake of Death
and I have no doubt you will find, if this treasure exists, it
is well guarded. Let then Snikhail, with that cunning
which is the nature of these worms, advise you how to
wrest your prize from its guardians. The ship has one
other guardian, for she is called *Cormorant*, and so comes
under the special care of these birds which, as you know,
though rarely seen at day-time, are masters of travel by
night. They also travel often in the dread hours when day
becomes night, which are an abhorrence to man. Under
the protection of these two guardians, I believe your quest
will succeed, saving only if that accords with the will of
the gods.'

Eusebius thanked Lord Sigurd for the splendid vessel,
and gave him, as a gift of parting, a heavy ring containing
a certain stone of many colours but none distinct.

'This stone,' he said, 'will serve you as a warning of the

approach of any danger. See now it is bright and shows many colours such as gold, blue, green, and a milky hue. Yet if danger approaches, whether weapon-danger or spirit-danger, the stone will lose all colour and turn dull. Then be on your guard and look closely into the hearts of your companions and think of your enemies and whether they do not plot some harm against you.'

'What might be the name of this stone?' asked Sigurd. 'Its like has not been seen before in this country.'

'It is called opal,' said Eusebius, 'and it is a stone which is spit up by certain rare birds before they die. These birds are called phoenix and on dying first spit up these stones and then burst into flames. From their ashes arises a new bird which immediately seeks the stone and expires if it cannot be found. There are in the world, I believe, only ten of these stones, and of the bird phoenix, it is thought there are but three yet alive in the country which is called Araby.'

So rare a gift greatly delighted Lord Sigurd, who put the ring on his finger straight away and informed the Lady Edessa and his whole company of its strange virtues. Eusebius was equally pleased with the mighty ship *Cormorant*, whose sides glittered with pitch and whose prow showed the gold, scarlet, and blue head of the worm Snikhail, from whose thin mouth jutted a forked and poisonous tongue.

Yet all did not immediately go well, for none of Lord Sigurd's men would of their own free will follow the Phoenician across the seas. He was no lord of theirs but a stranger, and they were men who served only one lord and could not switch their allegiance to another. Sigurd hoped that Swen of Wodestrund would volunteer to go with the stranger on his quest, for he was often fretful and sour of humour for lack of employment in arms. But he would not go nor any of his men. Six of those, however, who had served under Harald the Hammer and who had recovered from their sickness said they would follow the Phoenician, and testified that, though strange and slightly built, yet he had a rare knowledge of the sea and a strong heart in peril.

'He shouts not in battle, but smiles,' said one, called Finn Longshanks from the length of his legs. 'Yet his smile is more deadly than many a man's battle cry. I would not feel shame to die on the same field with him.' Others spoke well of the Phoenician, but still only ten of forty needed would follow him.

Then Lady Edessa, thinking of that Cup which Eusebius sought, and that if such a magic vessel existed it would be worth having some claim upon it, proposed that her son Knute should sail with Eusebius. He had never yet been on a sea voyage of any note, though he had whet a sword at the age of twelve in warfare with the East Vikings. They, however, are no great opponents, having turned more to raising corn than sacking forts and hunting the boar.

The boy was at this time drawing fast to manhood, being fifteen and of promising size. He had killed wolf and boar and wrestled well. Being not yet of a man's full age, he would not contest with Eusebius for the captaincy of the ship, but being son to Lord Sigurd, many men who loved his father would follow him.

Knute himself was hungry for the adventure and would not rest by day or night until Sigurd had given him permission to go. Then he would not rest by day or night until *Cormorant* had slid out of the fjord headed west to the White Island two days' voyage distant. With Knute came thirty good men, each with corselet, war axe, buckler, sword, spear, and helmet of iron – and so was the ship's company complete. Eusebius had also his special servant, that same Eric the Lame who had first seen the ship of

Harald the Hammer as it approached the fjord and who had also accompanied the Phoenician on the great wolf hunt.

Though others offered themselves as war servant to the Phoenician, he would choose none other than the broken man who had not before been to war. For his part Eric the Lame was overjoyed at this chance to at last serve on a vessel of war and show his mettle. There was nothing he would not do for the Phoenician, whom he now trusted completely. Men said it was wise of Eusebius to win the loyalty of one man by granting him so great a boon, for he had no kinfolk among the men on board.

When *Cormorant*, to the sounding of war horns and the beating of swords on shields, had passed down the gut of the fjord and out to the sea, and the rowers had begun to settle down to a good swing at their sea tools, Eusebius set the proper watches for the sea, dividing his men into two parts – the one under his direct command and the other under that of Finn Longshanks, who had been selected pilot, for he knew the approaches to the shores of the White Island.

Knute, son of Sigurd, Eusebius kept in his own watch so as to be able to instruct him closely in the skills of the sea, of which he was master, as he had promised his father. One watch would serve at the oars during the first half of the night, and the other during the second half, for it was intended that *Cormorant* should travel through night as well as by day, though it was more often the custom to let a ship drift at night and rest the rowers and the men.

To time the watches, a water clock was used. In a tub of water a vessel was set having a small hole pierced in the bottom. This first floated for a while but then, the water coming in, began to sink. When it had sunk, that was one period of the watch, of which ten made the whole.

This same water clock was used to see that each man stood only a fair time at the steering oar, where the labour was heavy. As for direction, it was a thing known to all men that stars set to the westward, and there is one star which stands always to the north. From two directions any other could be established, though on cloudy nights these aids were not available and so a good pilot worked with the direction from which the waves came (if this could be established) or from the flight of birds at dawn or dusk (if near land). Beyond these, they had no aids.

The watches being set and the headland cleared, a little wind came up from the east. This gave great cheer to all aboard, for the wind from this quarter was called the Sea Lord's or Viking's wind, since it would blow them from their lands to others which lay to the westward. The great oars were taken aboard, except the steering oar, and the sail set on its straining mast. *Cormorant* now sped prettily through the water, the sunlit spray splashing from her bow and sides and leaving behind her a wake of roiling silver bubbles and eddies. That this favourable wind should appear so early in the voyage was taken to be an excellent omen and a mark that the gods had looked favourably on the sacrifice of three ravens offered just before the start of the voyage.

A chart, drawn in blue dye obtained from acorns on a large piece of goatskin – the gift of Sigurd – was now produced by Eusebius, who summoned Finn Longshanks to tell him all he knew of it. This chart showed not only the White Island but also beyond it another smaller island.

'What is the name of this one?' asked Eusebius, pointing to the smaller island.

'It is called Last Island for the reason that there is no land beyond for as far as men have ever travelled and returned. The winds are for the most part from the west.

49

Therefore men can row against the wind as far as they dare and then be certain of returning by raising sail and running eastward before the wind.'

'And Last Island itself; have you or others you have heard of been there?'

'I have not been there myself,' said Finn. 'But the father of one of the men aboard was there.'

'Which man is that?' asked Eusebius.

'Vrilig – he with the red hair and beard,' said Finn. 'His mother was a Geat.' He said this because the Geats were reckoned to have special powers to penetrate the future and were also lucky.

'I will talk with him later,' said Eusebius. 'Now tell me of the White Island. Are the shores high or low, and is there an abundance of places to run a ship into and anchor, and are the people hospitable or warlike, and what are their weapons?'

'First as to the island, it is called the White Island because on the southern side are many cliffs of a height of three ship lengths or more which are of a soft white stone. But on the east side, which we will approach, the land is low and full of rivers and marshes in which there is a great multitude of wild fowl. The people who live here are of a strange sort, dwelling in small round huts made of reeds, and catching geese, ducks, moor hens, bitterns, and other sorts of birds on which they feast. They do not know the meat of animals, for there are no animals that can live in these wild marshlands. They are skilled fishermen and skilled boatmen, but not warriors, for on the appearance of our longships they quickly flee into their marshes and fear to fight.

'Farther to the south and still on this same coast, there is a big river called Tames. On the north bank of this river are these same marshlands of which I spoke. But on the south bank the land is higher and here are open leas and also some woodlands and plenty of deer and wolves and boars. The people live here under chieftains and in houses of wood, strongly built like our great halls and most often on hilltops. They fight well and use axe, sword, and spear but lack armour.

'They love to fight in open country and for this purpose have a kind of war cart, drawn by two horses, which is called a chariot. Two men fight in this, one to drive the horses at great speed and the other to use sword and spear. On the wheels of these chariots they fix knives to cut down those who try to climb on them.'

'What do these people call themselves?' asked Eusebius.

'Brythons,' said Finn.

'And their tongue?' asked Eusebius. 'What language do they speak?'

'They do not speak any tongue known to us,' said Finn. 'Not one word of theirs has any meaning for us. I have heard however that they are kin to certain tribes that live in the land of the Franks. However I have neglected to tell you that the greater part of their country was at one time conquered by people from the south who called themselves Romans and were great fighters and also builders. They built houses of stone of splendid size. But these have now all gone many, many years ago. The Brythons themselves do not live in these houses of their conquerors but fear them, believing, or so I am told, that the spirits of their former masters still dwell there. Perhaps you have heard in your country of these Romans?'

'These people are known throughout most of the world and were, as you have said, at one time great fighters and builders but have now fallen on slack times through quarrels in their army and the luxury of their living.'

'The fireside destroys the warrior, as every man knows,'

said Finn. 'At what place on this island would you desire to make a landfall?'

'I would desire to go up that great river of which you speak and which you called Tames,' said Eusebius.

'That is well,' said Finn. 'A day's rowing up that river there is a town of these people, ruined now, I believe, yet still containing a few inhabitants. It is called Lug's Dun; that is to say, the fort of Lug, who is one of their gods. There would be a good place to start looking for this Cup you seek. Other treasure may be found also. These Brythons were so long ruled by the Romans that they have forgotten the arts of the soldier. Much plunder may be had among them but, alas, no glory. Knute, son of Sigurd, will come back from this voyage with nothing to sing about in the Great Hall when the honey beer flows and the harpist plucks his pleasing strings.'

'I have come here not for glory nor for treasure, save only that one Cup which I seek,' said Eusebius. 'Are there any hazards about the coast of the White Island of which we must beware?'

'If it is your intention to approach that river called Tames, there are many ship-destroying sand banks to be avoided by running cunningly among the channels between them,' said Finn. 'On the southern coast there was a brazier kept lit since the days of the Romans to guide ships there, but since we are not to go to that coast, it is of no use to us.'

'No such brazier marks the mouth of this great river?'

'None,' said Finn. 'If black night stands guard upon that coast when we approach, we must keep off until the warmth-giving sun has risen.'

'It is always prudent to do so,' said Eusebius. 'Let us hope we make our approach by day.'

Chapter 8

That evening of the first day at sea Eusebius sent for the boy, Knute, who had during the day served his turn at the oars (the wind having fallen in the afternoon) and bid him make his bed beside him. 'I will teach you such things as may benefit you and will not forget to reward you for deeds of merit which you will undoubtedly perform,' he said.

'I will be grateful for what you can teach me and will do whatever you command,' said Knute. Although he had not yet the hardness of muscle which men achieve from the beating of the days upon their flesh, he was strong and of good courage – tall, broad-shouldered, and fair-haired, his hair being held in two thick braids which he wore over his chest, as was the fashion.

He had good armour of ring mail and that sword Scyldath, that is to say, Son of Death, which although not made by the Geats (greatest of swordsmiths) was forged by Beltin of the Ring Danes for their King Hrothgard, who lost it with his life to Edinth, King of the Swedes, at the Battle of Hroness. The loss of the sword in that battle produced that saying among the Danes that it is evil to meet the Swedes near the Whale's Nose – that being the meaning of the word 'Hroness', or in olden style, 'Hrondenissa'. Edinth, King of the Swedes, gave the sword to his own son Soegaard, who was drowned, as all men knew, in the Swede's Gate which divides the land of the Danes from that of the Swedes. Scyldath did not suffer its master's fate, to lie in the cheerless ocean, but was saved by Throweta, armourer to Soegaard, and then given to Sigurd of the West Vikings, who gave it to his son Knute for his first venture over the unknowable sea. It was a hammer-beaten blade of dark appearance with a cast of blue in the darkness and edged with skill by Beltin. The hilt had set in the end a bloodstone of great size and the handgrip was overlaid with twisted golden wire which would not slip during the sweat of battle.

Knute also had, as a gift from his father, Manguard, the great shield, heavily bossed and edged with the black iron of the Swedes, which will scarcely rust even if wet by the salt sea.

On that first night of the voyage then, the sky clearing, Eusebius revealed his star lore to Knute; how one star might be found from another, the names of those stars which formed groups in the black sky, and the names of those which move quickly across the sky and which are called, one the Fox, another the Hound, and another the Flame.

'Each star except those few which move faster keeps its own position in the sky,' said Eusebius. 'Each moves as in a well-trained battle host from east to west, neither falling behind nor catching up with those ahead. That this should be so is certainly a great marvel, and I have heard many reasons given of which two only are worth considering.

'The first is that the sky itself is not of air but solid and the stars are but bright points, like mountain peaks, on this solid sky which entirely surrounds the earth. If this were so, then plainly these mountain peaks or stars would keep their proper station and not change distance apart from each other.

'But the second explanation seems to me more likely and it is that each star is a sun in the sky, or perhaps a moon, and all are entirely still but seem to move because it is our earth which moves. So a man, galloping on a horse, looking to right or left finds the trees and rocks flashing by him though he knows that the truth is that the rocks are still and the trees also and only he moves. As for why sun, moon, and those other few stars move faster than the rest of the host, the reason may be that they are closer to us, and so seem to move faster. That this may be so is supported by the fact that the sun heats the earth, being closer, but no heat comes to the earth from the glittering stars.'

'Nor have I felt any warmth from the passing of the moon,' said Knute.

'The moon is perhaps of ice and the sun of fire,' said Eusebius. 'It is certain that the light of the moon is cold and that of the sun hot. The moon certainly has at times the appearance of ice. And yet what a man sees is often a deception and at times I have thought that the moon contains lands and oceans as does the earth.'

So they passed the time in profitable talk and when the last repast of the day had been eaten – before the west-ward-wending sun had gone – Eusebius passed among the men of the boat and spoke to each one of them so that they might know him more familiarly and he might know them. Some hoped that that night he would heave-to and let *Cormorant* lie sleeping upon the dark ocean as do other birds. But he, having closely questioned Finn concerning the distance to the White Island, preferred to continue voyaging through the night, calculating that the ship would then be off the mouth of the great river Tames by midafternoon of the following day, and they could then enter the river before nightfall, putting behind them those shoals which lay about to ensnare ships. Eusebius himself took his turn at the steering oar, which duty he divided with Finn, the pilot, and held his west-going course by the light of first one star and then another until the stars were drowned in the light of the new day.

When the Phoenician had finished his watch, which lasted until dawn, Knute rose and brought him meat and wine. This he ate seated on the stern of the vessel. As he was eating, he beheld on the steering side of the longship the mighty rising of a hron or whale in the seething ocean. Up rose the hron and blew his salute to the new day and then, remaining but a little below the surface, swam strongly toward *Cormorant* and slid under her black hull so close as to nudge the vessel in passing.

Then the hron dived and came to the surface some distance off and several times made this same passage under the ship before departing with a salute of his mighty flukes.

'Surely this is the best of omens,' said Knute, 'for that same sword which I carry, Scyldath, was won by Edinth, King of the Swedes, at the Battle of Hroness or the Whale's Nose (from the promontory of land on which it was fought). And the Swedes, as all the world knows, are close kin of the West Vikings.'

All agreed that this was indeed a good augury for the success of the voyage and praised Eusebius for bringing them successfully through the hag-ridden night. Nor did they forget to speak loudly in praise of Snikhail, that cunning worm, that had with its fierce regard frightened off such spirits as might have overset the ship during the night for spite.

There was that morning no wind, however, and the men were set to the oars, the sail having been lowered and carefully stowed beneath the rowing benches. Knute beat the rowing time for them upon his shield, making it ring with each blow of his excellent sword. Then, after a little while, when their muscles had awakened from the night's rest, they sang the 'Song of the Out-Goers'.

The cunning of this song lay in that the great oars were dipped with certain repeated lines, and also the men were put in excellent humour. So the morning passed pleasantly and when the sun hung hesitant in the sky at midday the Phoenician, in his bright-coloured cloak, showed his art in navigation. He marked the shadow which the mast threw across the vessel and upon the ocean and marked also that angle which the mast made with the waves. Then he told Finn to steer a little more to the left or southward, saying that if the map of the White Island was properly drawn, this course would bring them more readily to the mouth of the great river which they sought.

'How can such a thing be known?' asked Knute. 'Surely the best that may be done is first find the island and then inquire of those we meet in which direction, to the north or the south, lies the great river?'

'From sun shadow and the waves I know that we travel westward,' said Eusebius. 'But the river lies from the mid-point of our voyage a little to the south of west. During the night we have been carried northward by the movement of the water, which it is said travels in that direction to a great sinkhole at the top of the world, down which it plunges, passing through the earth and emerging from a fountain in the south of the world. This accounts then for the movement of the water northward. But I would very much like to journey northward to see whether there is indeed a sinkhole at the northern edge of the world, down which the great oceans swirl in dreadful fury.'

The thought of such a voyage made Knute stare at the Phoenician. 'For my part,' said the boy, 'if you went, so would I follow, sword in hand. But if you asked my advice, I would say that such a journey would be folly.'

Finn Longshanks at the steering oar, his great shoulders straining like a bull at that massive timber which alone controlled the direction of the ship, laughed aloud and said, 'Were it not for folly, life would hold no joy. Guided by Snikhail and Cormorant, I would gladly sail down that sinkhole and out of the fountain at the other side and face that terrible dragon who lives in the waters at the centre of the earth and whose name must not be said lest it brings bad luck on all within hearing.'

The position of the ship having been fixed, Eusebius instructed Finn to show to each man who took the steering oar the angle which the ship must make with the waves and warned that the sun must be allowed to make its path across the track of the ship from lading side to the steering side, and the ship was to be handled accordingly. He then wrapped himself in his many-coloured cloak and slept in the stern of the vessel. The men meanwhile (those who were not at work on the oars) amused themselves with gambling with dice for those spoils (not yet gained) which they believed would certainly fall soon into their hands.

Others played guessing games asking such riddles as 'What is born in the air, lives upon the ground, has neither arms nor legs, and yet is strong enough to break rocks?' to which the answer is 'Water'. Also, 'What cannot live without light and yet is destroyed by light?' to which the answer is 'A shadow'. With such amusements did they pass the time until, when the sun was in the last quarter of the sky and had crossed to the right hand of the ship, the lookout, embracing the neck of the worm Snikhail cried, 'I see gulls fly westward and a low cloud which does not change its shape.'

Quickly Eusebius was awakened and given this report, and he went himself to the lookout's post behind the grim head of Snikhail. 'It is land and we will make that coast in an hour,' he said. 'Now, Finn Longshanks, ply your skill with the sounding stone to bring us in safely past the sand banks you say guard the mouth of that river called Tames.'

Finn then went forward, and swinging the sounding stone on its line of rawhide, let it fall into the sea and called the names of the knots (set cleverly at certain distances upon the line) that sped through his fingers. The last knot that passed was the knot Otter, making a depth equivalent to the length of the ship beneath their keel.

'Drive on,' cried Eusebius. 'The tide favours. We will make the river before sunset. And those of you not at work at the oars look to the weapons. He lives in peace who looks for war.'

At this the Vikings grinned, for they looked not for peace which is tedious to all but women, but for war and the spoils of war.

Chapter 9

Now Snikhail, that guardian of *Cormorant*, did his best work, spying out with his cunning the sloughs of soft mud, the ridges of sand or shells, and of hard rocks that, unseen below the surface of the water, sought to entrap the Viking warship. Finn also used his skill with the sounding line, and Eusebius himself took the steering oar, but needed another to help him because of the fierce set of the current among the shoals, which came from many quarters and in quick succession.

This web which the water wove could not be seen (save by Snikhail) but only felt, and it happened often that with the steering oar set to starboard the current, coming suddenly from a contrary quarter, sent *Cormorant* swerving to the lading or larboard side. Then quick work was needed at the steering oar to prevent the ship being grounded upon a shoal. So Eusebius called Knute, that stout son of Sigurd, to help him with the oar. But if it were not for the cunning of the Worm, the ship would many times have been grounded, and once aground, must lie helpless for twelve hours open to attack by weather, by water, and by whatever enemies might beset them from the land.

They caught indeed the last of the tide flow, just sufficient of it to bring them into the mouth of the Tames water, whose marshy banks, touched here and there with the green flow of spring, seemed like threads of emerald and brown far away to the right and left of them. To the left, beyond these marshes, they could see low hills rising in the dying of the day, their western flanks stained gold by the setting sun; the eastward side plunged already in boding gloom.

In the valleys between these hills, a tiny light glimmered here and there, as from a single house. And on the summit of one hill, near the river's edge on that side, they beheld a large building of white stone, with many pillars before it and many oblong windows; also an expanse of terraces so large that they could be seen even at that distance and in the dying light. But from this building, in which the great hall of the Lord Sigurd could certainly have been contained, there came not a single light, nor did any move about its deserted terraces.

To the right, that is on the northern side – which quarter is especially under the protection of the god Thor, that lover of thunder and of storm – lay only the empty marsh, showing here and there a glitter of water stained by the setting sun, and now and then a tuft of some growth which, also catching the rays of the sunset, seemed to be afire. No craft came to meet them, no voice hailed, no homing bird flew close to the ship. They were alone then on an empty river in an empty land and with the day itself dying.

This silence produced a feeling of unease among the Vikings. Men looked at each other, saying nothing, for it is the part of a man to be lavish with his courage and a miser with his fears, keeping them to himself and well hidden from all eyes. All that was to be heard was the splashing of the oars in the darkening water and the shout of Finn as he made his soundings: 'The knot Otter ... the knot Otter again ... between Fox and Otter ... the knot Fox ... it deepens here ...' and so on.

'Blow a blast upon the war horn,' cried Eusebius. 'Let it be known that we are here.'

Then Vrilig the Geat, he of the red hair and red beard, took the war horn and blew three mighty blasts on it which first seemed to paralyse the whole world, and then set a cloud of birds whirring out of the marshlands, their wings beating the air and their voices raised in a clamour of fright. These birds settled down again to their nests after a while and once again that same silence descended over the whole area. Though they strained to hear an answer to the war horn, none came.

'The day is spent,' said Eusebius. 'We will anchor here in midstream for the night and then tomorrow continue on up to that town you say lies but a little way from the mouth of the river. But I have never known a country more deserted, except those that are afflicted by some pestilence.'

So the anchor stone was got out, the great sail taken down, and torches set at bow and stern to give warning of any attempt to reach them from the shore. Watches were established for the night and an evening meal cooked on the iron pots of the vessel. Some baited hooks and caught a quantity of eels, but these were allowed to go free, being brothers to Snikhail. A large flounder was also caught and then two smaller ones and a salmon, and these served to round out the dinner of deer meat and dried oats with which they were provided.

After dinner, when the moon (timorous sister of the sun) rose over the river's mouth, wetting the land with her light, Eusebius questioned Finn Longshanks and Vrilig again about the White Island and its peoples. It was certain, they said, that the people lived under chiefs and had kept many of the ways of the Romans, their former conquerors, who were long gone from the land. They were not warlike, not given to sea-roving and raiding, and Vrilig had heard they were often attacked by the Saxons and

Angles living to the south and east of them across the water.

'Some also of the Danes have been known to come pillaging here and with great profit,' said Vrilig. 'It is a pity indeed that we have not three ships, for we could take back great spoil to the honour and enrichment of our lord. Not only have these Brythons quantities of gold of their own, cunningly worked, some like fine netting and some overlaid with many colours which they call enamel, but also their former lords, the Romans, left many treasures behind.'

'That is true,' said Finn. 'I was here before and in the same river, and I now remember that house which lies to the south side of us. It was erected by the Romans, but the Brythons will not live in it, saying that the ghosts of their former masters still occupy the place. There is said to be a great treasure buried under its floor which is of square stones, some white and some black and forming a strange design.'

'What sort of treasure?' asked Eusebius.

'That I do not know,' said Finn. 'Perhaps dishes and other women's things in gold and silver. And cups – some jewelled maybe.'

'I would visit that place this night,' said Eusebius, his interest aroused on the mention of precious cups. 'It is no profit to lie here sleeping away the hours when we have come for a particular purpose.'

'Agreed,' said Vrilig.

'Nothing is simpler,' said Knute. 'The distance to the shore is scarcely a hundred paces. We can swim swiftly with our weapons and be ashore in no time at all.'

'And would you really take Manguard, that great shield of yours, and swim with her?' asked Eusebius. 'No. If we take weapons, we cannot swim. The river is too deep for wading. And if we move the ship to the shore, be sure that we will be seen. There is no such thing in all the world as a place which is not watched by someone.'

They held council what they should do and Vrilig with Geatish cunning proposed a plan by which they could move the ship to the shore unseen. His counsel was that they should place upright in the river two of the great oars of the long ship, one at the prow and the other at the stern. On these they should then fasten the torches which now were fastened to the prow and stern of the ship. Then they should, making the least possible noise, allow *Cormorant* to drift backward downstream for half a mile and then bring her to the shore. Those ashore seeing the torches burning in the middle of the river would think the ship still moored there. Watchers would keep that place under scrutiny through the night and meanwhile the Vikings could slip ashore, visit the building of stone standing so lonely on its hill, and capture a hostage or two who would certainly be of service to them on the following day.

This plan seemed good to them all, and everything was done as proposed and without the least difficulty. Soon *Cormorant*, having drifted away from her anchorage, was turned around and headed downstream a little way and then brought into the bank exactly opposite the deserted place (which Vrilig said was called a villa in the tongue of the Romans) on its hill. Here *Cormorant* was hidden beneath the branches of four large willows and a guard set to take care of her. Then Eusebius, with twenty men, slipped over her side, all armed and eager for danger. This party Eusebius divided into two groups and put the other group under the command of Finn Longshanks, telling him to circle to the south of the building and enter it from that side – timing his entrance so that Eusebius and his party would enter from the north at the same time.

Eusebius kept Knute with him, that young warrior having with him his great shield, which he was determined to carry on this first venture outside his own lands.

The two parties then went their ways and having gone but a little distance, that of Eusebius found an excellent road, though overgrown with wild growths, leading up to the villa. This however he spurned to use, for the road went up the ridge of the hill and would have made all visible to watching eyes.

Instead, he took a rough route through many stones and boulders following the bed of a small stream which flowed down toward the Tames. Here last year's bracken stood still waist-high, and the ground between the boulders was overgrown with brambles so that they moved but slowly. Yet they did so with little noise and came at last to the head of a little cleft and found looming against the sky before them the mighty white pillars of the villa.

Now (having climbed out of the little valley) they entered a garden, but one so ill-kept that it seemed but the wilderness, slightly groomed. There were pathways through places which had once been beds of flowers, and these pathways were made out of flat and polished squares of marble. Here and there, moving in silence and in wonder (not to say fear), they passed an overgrown fountain, standing in the middle of a stone basin and clogged with mud and with the leaves of many an autumn. Some of the fountains were carved in the form of beautiful women, pouring the water from pitchers into the bowl or bath in which they stood. Others were in the form of gods, some of human shape but with the legs of bulls or perhaps of goats, and others having the legs of men but the heads of bulls.

These marvels were not lost on the Vikings. They were by no means sure the creatures were carved out of stone.

65

They thought they might be creatures turned to stone by the evil gaze of trolls. So, passing them, they fingered their amulets against such evils – the Broken Cross of Thor which guards against the sorcery of women; the iron ring of Odin, sure warder-away of any evil thing that lies in wait for the lucky possessor of this excellent amulet.

In places they came to groves of little trees, once perhaps trimmed to pleasing shapes but now grown utterly wild, their ragged branches gesturing against the stars. Elsewhere they found other curious things – a large pool or bath of stone, full of foul water and weeds; a house with pillars instead of walls, supporting a round roof and containing again one of these stone figures, shamefully naked.

'We are without a doubt in some accursed place,' whispered Knute when the party came to a rest. 'Let us get out of here lest we ourselves be turned into creatures of stone, to stand forever exposed to wind and rain.'

'That is good counsel,' said another. 'You will not hear me complain in any battle, but I fear at any moment to make my last step in warm flesh.'

Seeing them thus uncertain and desirous of returning to their ship to try again in daylight, Eusebius called Eric the Lame to him. 'What say you?' he asked. 'Do you fear also to be turned to stone the next time the moon slips behind a cloud?'

'I fear indeed,' said Eric. 'But I will be the last man to turn back. Indeed, though I fear, I will not turn back unless you command me.'

'Learn courage then, you others, from him whom you call a broken man,' said Eusebius. 'These things you see about you are not done by sorcery but by the skill of men, for in the same way that the Geats can fashion a fine blade of steel, so the Romans have among them those who can fashion from stone a fine wrought man or indeed any other figure. And all these figures you see were made from stone long ago by these Romans.'

So, being rested and encouraged, they went on, not forgetting that they were to meet with the party of Finn at the villa and it would be shameful to be last at that meeting, even if it should prove a meeting with death. Then they came to the large area of marble terrace before the villa, clean of weeds, well-kept and gleaming in the moonlight which now shone full down upon the whole place. This terrace led to a flight of steps, perhaps twenty in all, at the top of which was a place of many pillars, like a walkway, before the house.

Seated at the top of the steps, well-exposed in the moonlight, was another of those stone figures carved by the Romans. It was the figure of an old man, bearded and clad in flowing robes, the head a little bowed, the hands placed in its lap. (This figure) the Vikings took to be the stone guardian of the place, and smarting under the words of Eusebius, which, though gentle given, still carried a sting, all moved on to the terrace in the moonlight towards it.

Then, as they approached, the man of stone moved, turned his head towards them, rose slowly, and his limbs, freed of whatever curse had been put upon them, walked down the steps towards the Vikings.

'Rex Tribonantiorum sum,' he cried. 'Qui adveniunt?'

And at the sound of this voice, all indeed among the Vikings were turned as it were to stone.

Chapter 10

The Phoenician was the first to recover his wits. He recognized the tongue in which the apparition had spoken to them and replied in that same tongue. He then turned to his companions and said, 'Courage. This is no enchantment. He is a man as we are – indeed a king of a people called the Tribonantes. Or so he says.'

'Beware of him,' said Finn. 'I have heard of these spirits that live in deserted habitations and are able to work their will on any who enter.'

But Eric the Lame seeing now, while all held back in fear, a chance for glory, uttered a cry and flung himself at the figure still standing statuelike upon the steps. At that moment there appeared from within the building, emerging from the darkness behind and between the ghostly pillars, a vast host of men, clad in armour, with helmets that gleamed in the moonlight and embossed shields that caught here and there a gleam of light. One of these, flying down the steps, flung himself, shield to shield, upon Eric the Lame, and the clang of those two metal bucklers meeting, broke the spell which had fallen over the sea warriors.

'Stay,' cried Eusebius above the tumult. 'We come in peace.' He held back his own host and crying aloud the word 'Pax' thrust himself between Eric and his foe. The strange king who had so amazed the Vikings now cried the word 'Pax' and the two fell apart, but Eric grinned for, though lame, he had laid open the cheek of his opponent with his sword.

An exchange now took place between Eusebius and this king in that language which the Norsemen could not understand and indeed of which they had not previously heard a word spoken. Then, to their surprise, this king spoke in their own tongue, though with hesitance and with words out of order and out of sound. Yet they understood him when he asked whether they were of the Saxon peoples or of the Angles from the lands beyond the river called Rhine.

'We are not,' said Eusebius.'We are from lands across the sea and to the north, though we have heard of these Saxons and Angles, who are however by no means great seamen as we are. For these Saxons farm only the lands, but these people whom I lead farm both the lands and the seas and are themselves lords of the sea.'

'And you are not one of them?' asked the king.

'I am not,' said Eusebius, 'but dwell among them and lead them at the moment. You, my lord, have said you are the King of the Tribonantes. Have you a title by which you may be called?'

'I am Arthurus, King of the Tribonantes, as I have told you, and Count of the Saxon Shore. Until the legions return I am all here that is left of Rome. I have the sign of the authority of the emperor and stand in his place.' He clapped his hands and from among the ranks of his band of war companions or guards, a man came, wearing in his helmet a plume made of some coarse bristles, dyed red. He was armoured, as were they all, but wore instead of leg wrappings like the Vikings, a short kirtle or skirt of leather strips that reached to his knees. He wore a breastplate under a long cloak of some dark colour. From under this cloak he took a sword contained in a scabbard so laden with jewels that they flashed cold fire in the moonlight. This he handed to the king, who held the sword in

69

its scabbard before him and said, 'This is Excalibur. Who holds it, rules here in the Brythonic Island.'

Seeing the sword thus displayed, the King's guard knelt before it and cried some words of reverence which sounded to the Vikings like 'Ave'.

Now it fell out that while the bodyguard of the king, numbering perhaps thirty men, knelt before the magical sword, the party led by Finn Longshanks reached the place, coming silently in the manner of sea raiders. They were in a position to take the king's men from behind and waited only the signal of Eusebius to do so, for he was not unaware of their presence.

Then Eusebius said, 'It seems to me, oh king who lives in a ruined palace, that you are badly guarded and are served only by ruined warriors. For behold, at this moment, while you show the badge of your power, my men have surrounded you. I have only to give an order and my sea wolves will tear your men to pieces and carry you away to their land, and with you this toy of a sword which you so greatly prize.'

The bearded old king turned his head, and his companions also, and saw that this was indeed true. Nor could they tell whether all the men who threatened them were to be seen or whether there were others hiding in the darkness.

Yet the king was not troubled, but maintained his dignity and said, 'You who travel with strangers did not come here to kill a king long past his joyous youth and take from him a sword of authority. You have, without a doubt, come in search of something else, and you say in peace. Do you come in peace?'

'I do,' said Eusebius, though this did not sit well with those who followed him.

'Then peace I give you,' said the king, making a sign of

magical import before him. 'Merlin said you would come, but from Gaul – and you are not from Gaul?'

'Who is this Merlin?' asked Eusebius.

'He is the chief of my councillors,' said the king. 'He has the gift to foretell the future. He is often away and is gone now to the western lands, but returns soon. Come within and we will talk of that which concerns us both.'

He turned and walked slowly up the steps toward the ruined palace and Eusebius followed, his own men with him. Not trusting themselves unarmed in a strange place, they carried their swords in their hands.

Chapter 11

In the receiving hall of Arthur's palace all was as ruined as in the grounds outside. Here there had once been great splendours to cause admiration throughout the world, but now Age, that tarnisher of all things, had worked its spoiler's will.

The furniture, cunningly contrived chairs and benches of fragrant woods, was broken and reft of gilding and of precious stones. No cushions of good sheep's wool lay on the seats but only split skins from which the stuffing peeked in mockery of elegance. Upon the walls, themselves of marble white, green-gold, and black, lay Time's mocking grime and the draperies which once clothed these kingly surroundings, now drooped like so many webs of cobs.

Some statuary stood around, figures of strange creatures such as flying dragons, winged lions, fish having claws instead of fins, and other dread beings both of lakes and forests. These were in better condition, as though attended by the palace servants. And there was also in the centre of this hall a vast table, round in shape and inset with many woods of rich colours. This alone was well-preserved, and the guardians of the king, coming before this table, bowed to it in reverence.

'Noble king,' cried Eusebius upon seeing all this splendour in tatters, 'what is the cause of this ruin? Have you no attendants and servants to clean up this palace and restore it to its proper beauty?'

'Let meat and wine be brought and let these voyagers from the sea be fed,' said Arthur. 'While they eat, I will speak of these matters freely, for Merlin himself told me of the coming of these men, though he was confused and said they would come from Gaul. Yet he well described their appearance and said they would be led by one who was himself a stranger to them.'

Food and drink was then brought but it was not set at the table for the companions of Eusebius to eat, but put before them in the many chairs and benches on which they sat about the reception room. The king's guard, meantime, at his order, withdrew to the farther end of the reception hall, the king alone sitting at that strange-shaped table which dominated the hall.

'The ruin which you see around you is the result of foul rebellion among those whom I trusted to defend me and my kingdom,' said Arthur. 'Scarce twenty short years have passed since smiling peace ruled in this land, and every man was safe in his house, and woman and child might venture abroad, even in the darkness of the night, without fear of hurt from anyone. Then had I a company of knights trained in every skill of arms, and eager to show their merit in any manly adventure. Among them I will mention Galahad of noble fame and Lancelot of the Lake, breaker of a king's heart and yet greatest of all men with lance or sword; gentle Gawain; ill-fated Balin and Balan, brothers in life and also death; Peleas of the Isles; and faithful Bedivere, the first and last of all my knights.

'But among them was one, of my own blood, Modred, who took arms against me, and in one great battle fought in the western part of my realm called Lyonnesse, destroyed all my kingdom and all my knights, though I myself slew Modred.

'Thus ended my kingdom and I, wounded heavily and

near death, was taken away to a certain island which lies to the west of this where all things hurt are healed by the very air. So I recovered of my wounds, and thinking of my people left without king or knight to protect them, returned though I might have stayed in that blessed island which is called the Land of the Ever Young.

'I found at my return all destroyed and in ruin; no knight alive of all my company and all my land filled with bands of thieves and brigands, and prey to those same fierce Saxons. None now would follow Arthur whom they called a defeated king, and few indeed would even believe that I was Arthur, but called me an old fool, uncertain in his wits. These few I have gathered around me knew of my former glory, but they are not enough to restore my authority in such terrible times. So I live in my old age with no more power than the robber bands against whom I must make war and the whole of my realm is open to invasion by sea pirates and others until one younger than I can be found to receive the sword. For it is a matter beyond dispute that the old who have seen the ruin of their plans cannot lead again the young in great undertakings.'

'You have no cause to complain if, as you say, all your knights died for you on that last battlefield,' said Finn Longshanks. 'Yet it is strange that you yourself should be alive. But I have no doubt that you find life a heavy burden to bear and show your courage in choosing to live when your war companions are dead, rather than to die as other men would have done in that last onslaught.'

Arthur looked gravely at Finn and replied, 'The easy path delights the child, the hard path justifies the man. The hardest path of all justifies the king who rules men. Since death is the common fate of all, it is surely no great virtue to choose an excellent death on the field of battle. Harder it is to choose to die of old age, serving others. Such a choice I made, and it was the choice of a king, who is at one time greater than all men, and at the same time, the servant of all men. Do you wish to speak further to this point, you of the yellow hair and long legs who have had scarcely thirty years use of the earth?'

But Finn said nothing.

'Tell me,' said Eusebius, 'who are these men, armed and armoured, who are with you now? They are not, you say, your knights of former times.'

'No,' said Arthur. 'They are but the remnants of my people whose fathers knew me and who have themselves, since that last battle, known only the life of fugitives and slaves. They are a band of men, some boys, some grey-beards, who came to me here on my return, seeing in me the last hope of peace for themselves. They find food and drink for themselves and for me, and wait, as I wait, for more men and more strength to re-establish my rule over this land.'

There was now silence while Eusebius and his companions considered the plight of the ruined king in his ruined palace and his ruined land. Certain thoughts occurred to Finn Longshanks who whispered to Knute, son of Sigurd, that had they not eaten meat with the old man, Knute might have for himself, won at the expense of a few blows of the war axe, a kingdom in this land to match that of his father in the Northland.

'There is wood yonder,' he said, nodding toward the king's bodyguard, gathered apart, 'scarcely worth the hewing of a single axeman.'

But Eusebius with a frown silenced the scheming Norseman and asked the king what was the significance of the strange carved figures about the hall, and also of that Round Table at which the king sat alone, not having invited any of the Vikings to sit with him.

'As for these figures,' said Arthur, 'they represent each those vices among men which in the days of my glory I conquered with the aid of my knights. Thus the winged dragon is Suspicion, that destroyer of all lands which, with a whispered word, turns every man's hand against his neighbour. And the winged lion is Calumny, stronger than any beast and quicker to travel from place to place than any bird; and the clawed fish is Jealousy, that lies silent as a carp in the water, but armed to tear apart all who come into contact with it. All these were once rife in my kingdom, setting man against man, knight against knight, band against band. All these I once, in my youth, overcame by teaching of Courtesy, Honesty, and Self-Sacrifice. And all these now, I must overcome once more.

'As for the Round Table at which I now sit alone, once there sat around it all those knights who supported me in my kingdom, and that none might find himself in the least slighted, I sat myself in the middle of the table so as to be as near to one as to all. There was the seat of Galahad, and there the seat of Lancelot, he of the Lake that came from Gaul, and there sat Gawain, and there brave Gareth, son of Lot and Bellicent. So they sat around, the ring to my shield of which I myself was shield boss and arm.

'Since they are dead, none now may sit here but I.'

Then Eusebius rose, and pulling around him that bright cloak he wore, strode to the table and quickly sat at the edge, opposite the king and said softly, 'Sir king, I bring you one new knight to take the place of those fallen.'

'Away,' cried Arthur, springing to his feet, and his men gathered around, weapons ready. But the men of Eusebius also rose and closed around behind Eusebius, and so they stood facing each other across that strange table shaped itself like a shield.

The Phoenician did not move, but continuing to sit at

the table said softly to Arthur, 'Sir king, I thought you said you had need of men to restore peace and good times to your kingdom. Here are men, each one of them worth ten of those who serve you now, for there is not a man at my back (save only the broken man and the young son of that famous warrior Sigurd) who has not reddened his sword a score of times in deathly combat.

'These men shall serve you if you wish, and I shall be your chief knight and warrior. I have no doubt that I will not be able to replace that man you call Lancelot of the Lake, who so nobly gave his life in that last great battle that you might live.'

Here Arthur blushed and bit his lip in some embarrassment and stood undecided before Eusebius, who was sitting in the seat of Galahad.

Emboldened by his leader's actions, Finn Longshanks, pushing aside with one hand one of the king's men, sat also at the table and said, 'I follow. I have no doubt the task will scarcely be fit for a man, but since my leader on this venture has offered his service, then I must also offer mine. I have no stomach, however, for beating peasants and old men and boys, and as for these Saxons who you say lay such waste to your lands, I will say nothing of them until I see them shield to shield. For the measure of a man is to be taken amid the battle's sweet red raindrops and not in talk in a mouldering hall.'

Vrilig also, pushing aside like Finn one of the king's men, sat at the table and said, 'I trust that the man whose place I take is worthy of my sword, which is made by Beltin himself and has topped many a head from ear to ear with hardly any work on my part.'

'You sit in the seat of Gareth of the Outer Isles,' said Arthur.

'I wish him joy in Valhalla then while I take up

his role here on earth,' said the Geat. 'Perhaps when I meet my own Weird, I will meet this Gareth and we can exchange a few pleasant strokes of sword or axe to see who among us is mightiest.'

'Where Gareth hath gone,' said Arthur gently, 'there is eternal peace, sweet music, and no combat among men.'

'Then will we never meet,' said the Geat, 'for I will not go to any such place, live or dead.'

'You will find yourself cast into the terrors and strife of Hell,' said one of Arthur's men, pointing his finger at the Geat.

'If I have sword and shield and perhaps one good comrade with me, then I will enjoy myself, whatever name is given the place,' said the other. 'What is terror for women and boys is but sport for men.'

Others then of Eusebius' band seated themselves one by one around the table, which was soon rimmed entirely with these armed Vikings, and Arthur, after his first protest, said not a word.

'Come, Sir king,' said Eusebius, 'we have not made our bargain yet. You have not spoken aloud plainly for all to hear. Do you wish the service of these men? Is that something which is desirable to you?'

'It is,' said the king. 'Yet my mind is troubled. I fear that I may be bringing in wolves to get rid of dogs.'

'That is true,' said Eusebius, 'but think also that you might be friend to the wolves whereas you might be enemy to the dogs.'

'Is it possible to be friend to a wolf?' asked the king.

'That is an ill-considered question, Sir king,' said Eusebius softly, 'for since wolves, moving together in bands, must be friend to each other and have trust in each other, it is plain that there is friendship and trust to be had among them.'

'But I am myself no wolf,' said Arthur.

'At this moment,' said Eusebius, 'you are yourself no king either. If there is friendship among us sea wolves or at least loyalty, then it is there for your use. If there is treachery among us, then it is there for your use also, for among those who are treacherous, there are always some to be found who will join your cause against their companions. Is not this so?'

'It is so,' said Arthur.

'Then be king, Sir king, and make your choice and aloud,' said Eusebius.

'I choose, then,' said Arthur. 'I have need of your swords. I ask your help.'

'It is granted,' said Eusebius, 'but upon payment of a price.'

'What price?' asked Arthur.

'First that you set aside a portion of your land and give it to these men to live in with their descendants as their own.'

'I feared such a price,' said Arthur.

'Who hires wolves had best have meat on hand,' said Eusebius smoothly.

'There is more to your price?' asked the king.

'Yes,' said the Phoenician. 'A certain Cup which I search and which is to be found in this kingdom.'

'What Cup is that?' asked Arthur.

'The Cup of Life,' said Eusebius.

'The Grail,' said the king, and looked at Eusebius in silence and with sorrow.

Chapter 12

The bargain was agreed in these terms: that Eusebius and his band should restore order to Arthur's kingdom, sending to their own lands for others to help if more were needed. When this was done Arthur would help Eusebius with advice as to where the Cup of Life, which he called the Grail, was to be found.

'I have heard of it myself,' said Arthur. 'I have not seen it. I make no promise concerning it.'

'It surprises me that having heard of it, you should not yourself have sought to gain it,' said Eusebius, his quick mind busy with secret thoughts and suspicions concerning the king, who had certainly, according to his own story, returned as it were from the dead after his last battle. 'Are you sure that it is not even now in your possession?'

'This I will tell you about the Cup before you even set yourself on the road to seek it,' said Arthur. 'No man may drink from it and remain the man he was.'

'There is some riddle here which I cannot read aright,' said Eusebius.

'Unravel me this riddle,' said the king. 'There can be no death without life, since that which dies must first live. Therefore life is the mother of death. Yet how can life be the mother of that which is the opposite of life? Have you any answer to this riddle?'

'All things are the parents of their opposites,' said the

Phoenician. 'That is a riddle for a child, and in our voyage here we amused ourselves with such riddles to pass the time.'

'Tell me,' persisted the king. 'If life is parent to death, is not then death also parent to life?'

But to this the Phoenician made no reply, his subtle mind (like to that of Snikhail) suspecting that more lay in the question than what was first understood.

The next day Eusebius, assisted by the king's guard, set about restoring Arthur's authority in his land to fulfil his part of the bargain. First, the officers of Arthur rode to the different hamlets and villages lying about, even as far as that city called Lug's Dun (now ruined and overgrown with thickets, and the lair of packs of wolves), calling on the people to send their leaders to Arthur's palace at Camelot. Some did and some did not, mocking at Arthur's power, and saying that he who now lived in the palace was an old dotard and no king of theirs.

To those who came, Arthur showed great courtesy, received them in his hall, promised them protection against the ravages of the Saxons and the bands of brigands who roamed the countryside, and gave them presents. He asked in return that they send one man from each ten of their number to serve in the king's host, and with that man supplies for his own needs and an equivalent amount for the king's use.

Some agreed. Some said this could not be done, for they had no food or weapons or clothing to spare. To these Arthur was inclined to show mercy and give them time to send the man and the tribute. But Eusebius counselled the king not to be so generous.

'What you ask,' he said, 'is but one-tenth part of what the brigands and Saxon raiders will take from them without your protection. Let them pay the small part lest they have to pay the larger and have no gain to show for the payment.'

'They are poor,' said the king. 'Let them be.'

'They are poorer in heart than in goods,' said Eusebius. 'Let me speak to them on your behalf.' He then turned to the host gathered in the hall and said in the Roman tongue, 'You have answered the king's call, but now some of you quibble about the tribute. There are some who, however, did not even answer the king's summons. I go with a part only of my men to punish these and get from them by force what they would not give to the king in loyalty. When I return, I expect that all will have supplied those men and goods of which the king has need.'

'You do not rule among us – Arthur is our king,' cried one among that sullen crowd.

'Who speaks?' asked Eusebius.

'Gaius, filius Ursi,' said a warrior. He was a man of great size, but carried only a spear such as is used for hunting wolf and boar. His black hair hung in tangles about his shoulders and he was clad in the skins of animals so ill cut that they scarcely fitted his frame.

'If Arthur is your king then why do you not serve him?' asked Eusebius. 'Your king is better served by strangers than by his own subjects. Are you not ashamed to stand there while the king's right is denied in every part of his country? Come with me and show yourself a loyal subject of your king, Gaius, son of Ursus – the Bear.'

So saying Eusebius left Arthur's palace with Eric the Lame and Knute and Vrilig and four or five others (leaving Finn Longshanks in command of the main body), and Gaius followed with some of his own men, for he was a chief among them. They went first to the stables to get horses and then by a road, once fair and now overgrown with brambles and grasses, to Kaintall where lived a certain chief, Hardmiget, who was among those who had refused to answer Arthur's summons.

This unruly chief had his encampment on the top of a hill with steeply sloping sides. There were three walls of earth piled up high around his encampment as a protection, and the house of the chief and those of his followers, built of sods of earth erected over a pit dug in the ground and lined with stones, were in the centre of the inner ring of earth walls. Before these houses were a number of tall poles. On one of these was a crucifix and on another was the skull of a horse, and on another the skull of a bear, for Hardmiget, with his followers, worshipped many gods – some long known and some but recently announced.

Also on poles in the same sacred area were standards with bronze eagles which Eusebius knew to have been the standards of the soldiers of Rome. The whole place was strongly fortified and there being no women or children to be seen outside the walls, it was plain that Hardmiget knew of their coming and was prepared for war.

Eusebius then took a careful count of his forces. He had of his own men but eight and Gaius had with him another five. This was no great number with which to storm so strong a fortress. Nonetheless, leaving their horses at the foot of the hill, they advanced to the first wall where they were challenged by a guard who made them depart, for his lord was hungry and would otherwise eat them for his breakfast.

'Bid your lord come and explain why he did not obey the summons of his king,' cried Eusebius in the tongue of the Romans. The fellow was surprised to hear this language from a stranger, and thinking that perhaps the Romans had returned to the land, ran immediately with a message to his chief. Shortly thereafter Hardmiget himself appeared on the walls, a man of frowning face and black beard which reached to his belt. He wore the armour of the Romans but no helmet, for his hair was so wild and uncut that none could be found large enough to fit his head.

Hardmiget looked about at the poor forces that followed Eusebius and, standing at the top of the wall, laughed in scorn. 'Is this all Rome could spare?' he asked mockingly, for he believed indeed that Eusebius had been sent by the emperor of that place. 'Be gone. You are but flies that annoy a horse which with one swish of his tail can kill you all. And tell that old dotard that I will soon put an end to his playing at king and sending to me for men.'

'I see that you yourself are strong,' said Eusebius. 'But I see also that you are fearful, for you have put around you and your few pitiful followers more protection than a snail – that most helpless of all creatures – fashions for itself. You have here three walls of earth and no doubt other fortifications beyond, and it is plain to me that though you may be a chief, yet you are chief only of cowards. It is a sad thing indeed to have come so far to see a strong man afraid.'

This mocking tone well suited the Vikings, who loved such sly sport, and Vrilig took up the play.

'It is certainly a surprising matter to me,' he said, 'to find so large a man greet his guests fully armoured as if what he lacked in courage he had to make up in metal coverings over his hide. Here it is scarcely midmorning and before us is a man so covered in metal that I can scarcely tell whether I see the front of him or the back of him. Perhaps he sleeps encased in armour lest some of his trusted followers plunge a dagger into him during his dreams – or some slighted woman give him a hard cuff during his slumbers, which would certainly make him squeal with pain.'

84

'By thunder, I will have the head of every one of you hanging dolefully on my walls while this day's sun still warms the ground,' roared Hardmiget. 'Your eyes, now so bright, will not see the last colours of the day.'

'And have you indeed three or four hundred men at your call to give us a little sport?' said Vrilig. 'If so I will look on you as a benefactor, for my ears tire of talk and my arm sighs for the song of the swinging sword.'

For answer Hardmiget blew a blast on his war horn and in a moment that rampart on which he stood was thick with men, some armoured, some not, and carrying a variety of weapons, though mostly spears and those short swords which are loved by the Romans and are called gladius.

'Give me room,' cried Vrilig and moved apart to have place to swing his great sword. 'Odin, watch closely now, for here comes a great feast of death.' The others also moved a little way from each other to have each the room needed for play with sword or terrible axe, but the men of Gaius stayed close together, this being their way of fighting with thrusting weapons such as short swords and spears.

However, before the onslaught Eusebius took that special weapon of his that killed from afar, and fitting a dart to the string cried out to Hardmiget, 'Ho, you worshipper of horses' skulls. See what I do to your smelly bones.' And so speaking he loosed his dart, which in a second struck one of the horse skulls and split it into two pieces (for it had been made fragile by many years in the weather) and it fell to the ground.

A groan of dismay went up now from the host of Hardmiget, and Eusebius fitted another arrow to his bow and turned that weapon full on Hardmiget himself. 'Make your farewell to life,' he said. 'The warm sun and pleasant air will soon cheer you no more.' But Vrilig, the Geat, rushed with a cry at Eusebius and knocked the weapon from his hands.

'For shame,' he cried, 'to spoil sport with killing from afar. Let them come on. You have no right to deprive us of this excellent chance for glory.'

Hardmiget then led his men with a shout from the wall and like a flooding of the sea overwhelming a few rocks, they surrounded the men of Eusebius and of Gaius. Now rang out the battle shouts and swords spoke with their bright tongues, shield clashed on shield, and men, hewn down, shouted to their gods of their coming.

Knute, son of Sigurd, having also taken a place for himself apart, fought manfully with that great sword, Scyldath, which hissed pleasantly in the air and reaped its harvest of crimson fruit.

But Eusebius, ever quiet in battle, sought out Hardmiget and found him already engaged by Gaius who, with a spear alone, had challenged that bearded giant. Even as Eusebius reached his side, Gaius was brought low by a stroke of the short sword of Hardmiget which caught him on the crown of his head. Then Eusebius moved in close with his own short sword and knowing the weak places of the Roman armour (which was indeed no new thing to him) slipped beneath a thrust of his enemy's sword and drew his own blade across the knees of Hardmiget. Hardmiget then leaped back, but Eusebius followed so fast that no advantage was gained by this leap. Hardmiget struck at the bright-coloured one who with his small shield readily fended off the ill-aimed blow, and thrusting his sword under his enemy's arm where the armour gave no protection, brought him to the ground and so dispatched him.

Then the Vikings saw something which surprised them and filled them with contempt. For with their leader gone, the men of Hardmiget did not fight on the harder, but rather shouted that he was dead and fled from the combat, chased by the men of Gaius but ignored by those who followed Eusebius, who would not deign to shame their blades by cutting down so unworthy a foe.

Much loot, however, fell into the hands of the Vikings, for they gained a great weapon hoard from the fallen and also from that fortified place called Kaintall which they had soon made their own, with all its store of food and many treasures. Although the people of this place lived in crude dwellings, little more than pits dug in the ground, still they had amassed from the deserted homes of their former overlords a great quantity of delicate cloths and of dishes and cups, of rings and bracelets, and armbands in copper, gold, and silver – some of them cleverly enamelled. All these then were taken to Arthur, and Gaius was left in charge of Kaintall to hold it for the king and at the king's pleasure.

Yet the force of Eusebius had paid heavily for the gaining of that place, for three of the Vikings were dead and three also of the men who followed Gaius would never more plant or harvest grain. The men of Gaius who were dead were disposed of in a horrible fashion, their bodies being taken and buried in the ground, and over the places where they were thus put (like dogs) were erected crosses made of wood which it was said would ensure that happiness in Valhalla, which they (nonbelievers in Thor or Woden) called at times Heaven and at other times Paradise.

But those of the Vikings who had died, that is to say Kirkgaat and Hradarda and Gnethfyth, who was a Swede, were taken back to Camelot and burned on a warrior's pyre, with their weapons beside them and their bodies loaded down with gifts from both Eusebius and the king. The flames roared loud in the east wind and the smoke of

87

the pyre rose mightily to the very clouds of the sky, and Finn and the others delighted to see so fine an end of their companions whom the Valkyries had selected to join the gods.

Chapter 13

This then was the manner in which with the aid of the Vikings (for without them nothing could be done) the rule of Arthur was restored over his subjects. That hardy group of Vikings had seen extended the king's authority northward of the Tames River in the lands of the marsh dwellers and southward to the sea and westward beyond the Great Plain amid the forests, and thus to the very margin of the place where on that island the earth is no longer white but is red. This place was called Lyonnesse and was in part heavily forested, and was in other parts wild moorlands covered by bitter shrubs whose ragged branches clawed blindly at the wind as it passed by.

This was not brought about without many feats of arms both by the Northmen and by those who now began to follow Arthur in greater numbers. For when Hardmiget was brought down by the sword of Eusebius, many who had been in fear of him now joined the cause of the king. Also many others, hearing of the might of the king's men, came to pledge their loyalty to Arthur so that day after day there were more and more groups coming to Camelot of the white pillars and pleasant terraces, bringing with them tribute and men.

Thus Arthur soon had about him a full company of warriors. The gardens about his palace were restored to their former grace, the rooms of the palace were also renewed, and much that had withered since that last great battle in which the king had lost the company of his Round Table was refreshed with new life.

All this greatly pleased the king, but the Vikings were not so well pleased at first. They found that they were not allowed to pillage and loot, taking to themselves the possessions of their defeated foes which they held to be rightly theirs.

'It is a matter known to all men that fighting is in itself an excellent diversion,' said Finn. 'It is a pleasure to me to hazard my life once a week or perhaps even more if I am lucky, in combat with brave men. But I find it hard indeed that I may not then, having defeated my foes, take that which was theirs and bring back as servants and slaves the dependents of those who have fallen to my war axe.

'No man is more generous than I. I have certainly given away to others the greater part of the gear and slaves that I have won in battles before coming to this island. But it is nice to be able to look upon shield, helmet, sword, or slave woman and recall with pleasure how these were won and what blows were given and taken in the winning of them.'

This same discontent affected all the men who followed Eusebius. They were accustomed to bringing all such loot to their lord, who in this case would be Eusebius, since he was their lord for the present time. In return he was expected to return much of this spoil to them at feasts and with it praise them for their valour.

But Arthur wished no such loot brought to him, though he did not object to the Northmen collecting the personal weapons of those they had killed on the field. Eusebius counselled him to hold a feast and reward each of the warriors with bracelets of gold and silver, and collars of gold and great shields, and such things.

'Is it not a sufficient reward for the men that they bring peace and security to these people and all men now bless them?' asked Arthur. 'Does it not recompense them for their danger and their wounds that they are well received wherever they go in the lands they have subdued, are invited to dine with this chief and that, and are everywhere treated as heroes?'

'Not in the slightest,' said Eusebius. 'Peace and security are not the things they seek, but praise and honour from their lord and rewards of such gifts as I have described to you.'

'Do they not understand that there are greater rewards than cups and bracelets and helmets to be had, after death, for the deeds they now perform?' asked Arthur.

'They do indeed,' said Eusebius. 'For when dead, they expect they will be honoured in Valhalla according to their valour on earth. But they need on earth their reward also. So prepare a great feast as I advise and give generously to each of them.'

Arthur, then, the forests and wild areas of his lands being now largely cleared of brigands, first held a great hunt at which deer and boar and bear were killed and then gave a lavish feast for all the company of the Northmen and those who followed Gaius. At this the meat was plentiful, there was an abundance of golden loaves and honey beer and wine also from the southern lands. There was also ministrelsy and song, and to each of the Norsemen he gave a great quantity of gifts from his own stores – helmets and swords, spears, axes, armour, cloaks, cups and collars of gold and of silver, and also plates of gold and bracelets of precious metals, armbands, and such things as delighted them. The minstrels sang the praises of these men, but not entirely to their satisfaction, the singers themselves having little aptitude in this most manly skill. Therefore the warriors sang their own praises, not forgetting to acknowledge the heroism of their enemies, as was fitting.

Then before venturing further in the subjection of the lands of the king (which formerly extended from east to west of the island and from north to south, except the lands of the wild Pictish tribes in the north) Eusebius sent back *Cormorant*, guided by Snikhail and under the command of Finn Longshanks, to get more men, for many of the Vikings had now fallen and their host was reduced to one half. The ship was laden with the treasures received from the king, for that wily man Eusebius knew how best to stir excitement in the hearts of the Vikings.

And so, within three weeks back came *Cormorant* with more warriors and with her another ship, *Black Gull*, of whom the guardian spirit was Grundath, that great dragon whose resting place is in the mountains in the interior of the lands of the Vikings, and whose breath produces the winds.

There were now in the Viking party, very close to a hundred men (for neither of those ships had sailed undermanned – such was the lure of the treasure). Eusebius divided this host into two groups, giving command of one group to Finn and taking command of the other himself.

To Finn he gave the task of guarding the lands already brought under the king's authority. He himself, with the second party, determined to set out for Lyonnesse in the western part of the island, travelling first along that river Tames for some distance and then, deserting the river, marching westward toward the setting of the sun. This would bring him to the island called Avalon where the Cup of Life was to be found, according to Arthur.

Arthur himself would not leave Camelot, fearing that if he did so, strife would break out among his newly pacified people. But he gave to Eusebius, to fulfil his promise, a map drawn by the wizard Merlin showing what road should be taken westward to Avalon and what hazards were to be met upon the way. This road passed through the Forest of Eppin, then the Valley of the White Horse, and then wound southward towards the Great Plain of the Stones; and thereafter onward through the Singing Hills and the Western Wilderness, and so to the lake in which lay Avalon.

'Even in the day of my knights,' said Arthur, 'none travelled this road from end to end. The Great Plain of the Stones is especially perilous. By all means cross this mounted on good horses and by day, for to be caught upon this plain at night is to be deprived of your wits – such is the evil power of those who formerly occupied this place.

'Also in the Singing Hills you will find a race of dwarfs, misformed and treacherous, who will beset you in their thousands unless you can by some means make friends of them. But if they know that you are from my court, they may let you by, for Lancelot in former times did them some service which they may remember. See, I will give you a ring which will serve to show that you are friend of Arthur.'

Then he took from his finger a ring of plain gold in which was set a flat red stone. On the surface of this stone were written the words 'In hoc signo vinces' with below them a cross. This Eusebius knew meant 'Conquer in this sign.' The sign he knew to be the same as was put over the graves of many of the men who died for Arthur. This sign interested him deeply and he asked the king its meaning.

'This sign stands for that Cross on which Christ, the Son of God, was crucified,' said Arthur.

'Is he not the same who drank from the Cup of Life and then was raised from the dead?' asked Eusebius.

'That is so,' said Arthur. 'But he was raised from the dead because he was God and not because he drank from that Cup which we call the Grail.'

'I think you are mistaken there,' said Eusebius. 'It is plain first of all that if he were a god, he could not be put to death, since the gods are immortal. Therefore he must have been but a man. Now if he were a man and dead, then he could do nothing for himself, for the dead are impotent. Therefore that which restored him to life must have been the Cup from which he drank. Also I believe I know more of these things than you do, for the land in which they happened lies only a little to the south of my own country, and I have made inquiries about this matter and it is clear that the ability to rise again from the dead lies in the Cup.'

Arthur appeared about to argue further on this point. But instead he shrugged, smiled, and said, 'None are so sure in argument as those who know but the half; none so hesitant as those who have been told the whole.'

This disturbed Eusebius, who began to suspect again that the king might be holding back something from him. He then pressed Arthur for more of the story concerning the magic both of the sign and of the Cup, but the king replied only, 'Seek and you shall find. That promise I am able to give you. But more I will not tell you, for it is not with words and with reasons that these questions are answered but by some other power not in the control of man.'

'The sign on the ring then contains some magic, though not as powerful as the Cup?' asked Eusebius, his sly mind questing for a hint of what the king might be hiding from him.

'Neither sign nor Cup contain any magic at all,' said the king.

'And yet this man whom you call Christ was indeed raised from the dead?' said Eusebius.

'That is so,' said Arthur. 'And this was done to show to men that death is not the end for man.'

'Only a fool would believe otherwise,' said Eusebius. 'But what interests me is not to die and go to another place, but to die and return to life here on earth, which I find pleasant and interesting, and I desire no other. It is for that reason that I seek this Cup.'

'Go then and seek it,' said the king. 'But I have already warned you that no man who drinks from it will remain the same.'

'As to that,' said Eusebius, 'if it is to be found, then I will drink from it.'

And so he left, having with him now as his lieutenant Vrilig, the Geat, and with him also, among his men, Knute and Eric the Lame. Vrilig he brought not only because of his prowess with the sword but also because the Geats have great skill with metals and control over metals, and Vrilig could best tell whether the Cup, once found, was the true vessel of purest gold and therefore the precious Cup which Arthur called the Grail.

Chapter 14

Before setting out with his band for Avalon, Eusebius
first gave orders that *Cormorant* and *Black Gull* should
move up the river to that place called Lug's Dun of which
he had heard. Finn had said it lay but a mile upstream, but
this was not so. A full day's hard work at the oars was
needed to bring the two ships to that place – once the
home of men and now the haunt of animals. Here however were stone jetties to which the ships could be moored
close to land. Here also were wells with fresh water. All
roads also led to this place, so it was easy to supply the
men with food and other needs, and there was a fort of
white stone close by the river in which the men could live
and from which they could control both the city and the
countryside.

This fort was a wonder to the Vikings, being round in
shape, the walls very thick, and pierced by slits of windows. Within the walls were storehouses for arms and
food and also stables for horses and living quarters for
many men. It was built by a great chief of the Romans
called Caesar. Such working of stone the Vikings had not
seen before, for they worked only in wood and metals
and bone. It was plain that each stone of the mighty walls
had been hand-shaped, and thus thousands of men had
been put to the work which otherwise would have taken
many lifetimes to finish.

'What a tedious task,' said Vrilig. 'To spend all your

life shaping stones! Certainly it would be better not to live at all.'

The city contained many streets which spread out from this fort of Caesar's like spokes from the hub of a chariot wheel. Along these streets, some paved with flat stones in which were worn the wheels of war chariots and of goods wagons, were the ruins of smaller houses, some of stone and some of wood. Roofs were gone, walls had partly fallen down. Masses of brambles and bracken covered the greater part of them, and through their floors (often paved with stone) sprang bushes and young trees – hawthorn, wild rose, beech, and ash.

Wild hogs grunted and snorted about the place in fierce packs. Even in the walls of Caesar's fort the nests of adders were found, and on a hill not far away (the fort itself was on a hill close to the river) where there was a temple, two wolves were killed by the men of Eusebius as well as a many-antlered stag.

The Phoenician, who found pleasure in all new things, spent two days in this city and found many marvels among the ruins. At one place, inside a ruined hall of stone, was a vast pool, filled with mud and slimy water, and in this pool, it was stated, men at one time bathed in great numbers for their pleasure.

There were also many temples to pleasant gods and goddesses, some of them of the warrior kind but most of them gods of peace, it would seem, for they were crested with no war helmet, nor carried they hammer or sword, but wore robes coming to their feet like women.

These gods the Vikings held in little regard and told each other that it was certainly because these Romans had worshipped such womanlike gods that they had at last been defeated in war. At one place, however, in a temple close to a number of larger but ruined houses, they found that same strange cross which was carved on the ring Arthur had given to Eusebius. But on the cross was the figure of a man, nailed, and in great pain.

This Eusebius examined in awe, for it was the first time that he had seen an actual representation of the death of that man who had returned to life after drinking from the Cup which he now sought. Certainly here was the strongest indication that such a man had indeed been put to death in that manner, and also that his death was fully understood in this distant island.

The Vikings were scandalized that any man should be killed in so ignoble a fashion.

'What kind of folk could have done such a thing?' they demanded of Eusebius. 'Surely the name of these people must live in shame forever to have killed a man in a manner in which none of us would even kill an animal. Will you not lead us against these people so that we may give them a taste of the edge of our swords for having done so horrible a deed?'

Eusebius then explained that it was the wish of this man that he should be so dispatched. They then understood that the figure was in truth that of Odin, who had wounded himself and hung himself for nine days and nine nights on the tree Yggdrasil to restore his waning youth, and had succeeded with the help of some magical runes he had managed to pick up from beneath the tree.

'It is Odin's cup that you seek then,' they told Eusebius. 'And this name Christ these people have is only a name in their language for mighty Odin.' They had noted the ring which Arthur had given Eusebius and which contained the sign of the cross. The Northmen were now glad to be venturing out under the protection of this sign, which they took to be the sign of Odin, or rather, the sign of the

Tree of Life, Yggdrasil. But unlike Eusebius, they were not anxious to drink from Odin's cup, as they now called it, and so after death return to life in this world.

'Valhalla is better by far than anything here,' they assured Eusebius. 'Who would want to linger on this earth, outside that Great Hall of the gods where the ale horn is ever full and the table groans with good meat?'

Good horses were now obtained (for there were many of them in that island, some tame and some in herds which had gone wild). Well mounted, they set out for the western part of the kingdom, first crossing the river to the south by a ford which they found close to the fort of Caesar.

Spring had now come fully to the land. Flowers of many kinds splashed the grasslands and hedges, and the low grass was prettily ruffled here and there by the warm western wind. New leaf was on every tree and bush, and birds sang in their piping voices from the depths of the woods and in the open spaces. The meadowlark fluttered up to the sky, there to sing his cheerful song and fall to the earth like a stone, and the wise plovers swooped and soared over the meadows calling to each other with grave notes.

Eusebius, according to that map which Arthur had given to him, followed a road built by the Romans westward. It was now little used, and so, like all their works, overgrown with grasses and new ferns. Yet under these, the road was sound and its track could be seen over hill and down valley, straight as a lance aimed at the sunset. Buttercups grew so tall on the way that soon the bellies of the horses were golden with pollen, which promised perhaps happier spoil, and so all were in good heart as they rode along.

By midafternoon they had entered a forest in which the trees first grew at some distance apart – great oaks and beech and larch and pines they were – and then closer and closer together with so much underbrush that were it not for the road they would never have been able to make their way through. But towards evening the road itself gave out. They found themselves entirely surrounded by thorny thickets and by ferns which grew waist high, while over their heads spread the huge and menacing branches of trees, moving a little forward and back again and then up and down as if to menace the warriors.

Silence fell on the party. At first they pressed forward using their horses to make a path. Then the hedge of brambles and of bushes beneath these mighty trees growing thicker, they were forced to cut a way on foot. Eusebius consulted his map, which showed that his path lay through the forest which was called Eppin. Yet the map showed a road going straight through.

'It is plain we have lost our way, my lord,' said Eric the Lame. 'Allow me to go back and search behind us, for we must have taken a spur of the road which was not completed. It is overgrown as you know with plants and weeds, and it would not be hard to take a wrong turn.'

'Go then and we will rest here awhile,' said Eusebius.

Then Eric set out, and the others dismounted under the spreading branches of a great oak, moss-hung and itself supporting gardens of plants in the crotches of its branches. A great fire was lit both for warmth and to scare off the wolf packs which they knew well loved such places, and meat was put to roast over the fire on a spit.

Four men were placed to guard the camp, for the light now was going from the sky and the mourning owls began to hoot about the treetops. In the darkness around the encampment eyes could soon be seen in pairs, peering at the fire and the men, and then disappearing in the black mystery of the night.

'I doubt we will see that broken man Eric again,' said

Vrilig. 'He was a hardy man to venture lone into this forest, which I believe to be enchanted, with the day almost gone.'

'No harm can come to him,' said Skathrig, who was one of the East Vikings, and held in much respect, for his mother had been a priestess of Odin. 'He has the mark of the troll on him and so those hideous spirits of the night will not hurt him.'

'That is true,' said another. 'He who escapes one of them, as he did at birth, is free from them all. Would you say those are wolf eyes that watch us from beyond the circle of the fire?'

'They are,' replied Vrilig. 'The eyes of the wolf, seen in the dark, are green fire, as all men know. Those of the forest cat are red, also those of the porcupine, while the eyes of the bear are white and far apart.'

'Those of the Forest People are dull like withered acorns,' said Skathrig. 'Their skin resembles moss and their hair is like ferns but of flesh. They will do no harm to any man if he will but say to them as follows:

> Moss-skinned thing let me by.
> See, my blood is red.
> You cannot drink it and live.

'You must then cut yourself and show red blood, for these people live on the white or pale green blood of trees and other growths. It is from them that the men are themselves descended.'

'I have heard that they talk very slowly and they think also with great pain,' said one.

'That is true,' said Skathrig. 'But whatever they tell you is true. They cannot speak falsely. But beware of telling them any untruth. Those who do, they smother to death in their mossy arms.'

Some more time went by with such uncomfortable talk. Here and there eyes of wolves, bears, and hunting forest cats burned in the darkness outside the circle of the fire-light and then were gone. Now and again the Vikings heard the howl of the hunting wolf, or perhaps (for one cannot always be sure of these things) the cry of the werewolf, that devourer of sleeping men whose size it is said exceeds that of a horse. When the sun was four hours set and Eric the Lame had not yet returned, Eusebius spoke of setting out to look for him, but his followers begged him not to do so but to remain with them.

'Evil has without a doubt befallen that broken man,' said Vrilig. 'He has perhaps met his Weird at the hand of some forest creatures. He may now be enclosed in the damp and airless trunk of some great tree, or taken down in some accursed pool by those creatures that love such places and charm men to their death by appearing to them in the form of lovely maidens singing irresistible songs.

'But you will find nothing if you follow him, and we will be leaderless. It is true that you are not one of us by blood, but since you are our leader, then it is your task to stay here. At dawn we will kill some small thing and I will read in its guts what has happened to that Broken Man for whom you have such an attachment. Meanwhile it behooves you to remain here.'

The others agreed that all that Eusebius might do to assist Eric the Lame was to blow several blasts on the war horn to bring him back.

These blasts, when their last note had died away, were answered by many more, from every part of the forest, some seeming distant, some near. It was plain that in that foul place the Norsemen were surrounded by the spirits of the Ignoble Dead who did not deserve to be taken to Valhalla.

They built the fire higher and slept, those who were not appointed to watch in its ring of light, with sword and shield close by. So they passed an uncomfortable night in the brooding and spirit-haunted Forest of Eppin.

Chapter 15

When Eric the Lame left to find the Great Road of the West, he hoped by all means to distinguish himself by being able to put the party on its proper track again. It was his wish (proper indeed in all warriors) not only to be the equal of all his companions but to outshine them; the more so since he had so long been scorned as scarcely a full man. He had done well in the fight with the warriors of Hardmiget and certainly no man could complain that on that field he had played the laggard's part. Yet he had not outshone the performance of his fellows. Now he hoped to be the means of saving his party, a feat which could by no means be ignored when the story was related in song in the Great Hall of Lord Sigurd.

He had set out on foot, for horse could not go faster than man, even a lame man, through the thickets. Nor was he clear of all fears, for he knew as well as his fellows that many foul spirits lived in such forests, and that mark which had been placed upon him might not defend him in every case. His shield he slung across his back, and carrying only his sword, which he used to cut his way, set forth.

It took little skill to follow the trail of the horsemen into the forest's depth while the light still lasted. But soon this was lessened and then, though the shapes of shrubs and thickets and trunks of hoary, moss-laden trees could for a while be made out, that broad track through them was not to be readily found, particularly where the bushes pushed aside had swung back into place and the elves (keepers of the forests) had raised again the trampled grasses.

It greatly heartened Eric to find out about this work of the elves, who are good folk and will certainly help any human they find in a forest, though they will first have their amusement with him. He caught here and there an elfin glitter in the thick growths and knew these shining creatures watched him. So, although now quite lost, his fears diminished, particularly when he recalled that elves were especially kind to those who were lame and those who had crooked backs.

To be sure of the protection of these graceful and beauty-loving folk, Eric now recited the 'Rune of the River Elves' to whom, as all men know, all other elves are related:

> Elfin folk like liquid light
> Ripple in the gloom of night,
> Tiny bells your voices seem
> As water clear in mountain stream.
> Stop your pleasant forest play,
> To guide this Lost One on his way.

When he had said this rune (which, unlike other poetry of his people, employed rhymes) he listened carefully for a reply and looked about with equal care. Then he saw ahead of him a little light, soft and pale, which increased and diminished and at times disappeared only to reappear again. He knew this to be an elfin light and moved through the thicket toward it, careful not to do too great damage to the bracken and undergrowth, which would certainly be lacking in courtesy to the elves.

The more he advanced, the more the light retreated from him, turning a little to the left or right at times, and leading along a small path which was used, no doubt, by elves and deer and other forest creatures.

The light, low to the ground, shone here and there on leaf, grass, and stem and led him ever away from the encampment of his companions, and away too, so he felt, from the Great Road of the West, which they sought to follow.

At last, having followed the light down a valley, across a dark and swift-flowing stream, and up this stream on the other side, the light disappeared. Now the Lame One found himself standing before the yawning entrance of a cave hung with dripping mosses and long creepers which, moving in the night wind, reached out to touch him with wet fingers.

A strange dwelling for River Elves, this seemed, and Eric thought that he must have followed after all the light of a gnome – cousin to the elf people, but who take care of all underground places. These he knew to be also good-hearted folk though more rough-spoken than the elves and not skilled, as were elves, in spinning cloth from threads of gold and silver – gnomes being for the most part workers in wood.

While he stood there uncertain before the gaping black-ness of the cave, a cold wind came down on him from the cliffs above, and with it several big drops of water, and taking these for a warning of danger, Eric unbuckled his shield from his back, put it upon his left arm, and with his sword ready, walked into that cave through the portals of mosses and creepers.

Within he saw for a moment nothing – no shape, or light, or anything standing still, or anything stirring. Indeed, all was dark as if his eyes had on that moment been pushed from his head. He listened intently but heard nothing and so said in a steady voice (deeming himself invisible in that darkness), 'Beware, whoever waits within, that you do not harm me. For I am Eric the Lame, a Broken Man, marked by trolls and to be hurt by none but men until my death. Therefore, whoever waits within, if you be not man, do not dare to cast evil words or looks at me. And if you be man, say so plainly – and whether you intend peace or war between us.'

No answer came to this and Eric was about to turn around, thinking he had mistaken the direction in which the light had led, when he saw, deep within the cave, a faint gleam which shone bright for a moment and then diminished and seemed to beckon him. Off he went towards it, and now the light no longer receded before him but awaited his coming. At last he reached it and found the light indeed came from a small lantern containing light-giving flies such as the elves use to guide themselves.

The flies being quiet, now gave but a dim light, but on being shaken up, which happened in a moment, glowed into a high blaze which lit the whole area nearby.

Then Eric saw that it was no elf or gnome that had led him there. For he who owned the lantern was a very old man with a beard that reached to his knees and long white hair that reached to his waist and was, in fact, hardly to be separated from his beard. His face was long and lined, his eyebrows thick and hoary, and he was clad in a robe of purple gathered at the waist by a belt of heavy gold.

This ancient man examined Eric gravely by the light of his buzzing lantern and said, 'Put up your sword, Northman. No foe is here to give you pleasant combat. What do you seek?'

'We are lost in the forest and seek the Great Road of the West to that part called Avalon,' said Eric boldly.

'You will not find that road again nor any road out of

this place unless I grant you leave,' said the ancient man. 'Come. Let us talk and eat together.'

Then he led Eric back farther into that dark cave and through a winding passageway down stairs and then up again, and then across a room lit with a strange grey light from below (for the floor of this place was light but the walls and roof dark). On they went into another dark way, very hot, and then into a vast hall, well lit with torches which flamed in bronze or perhaps golden holders fixed to the walls. This hall was sumptuously furnished – the walls covered with tapestries and satin and silks.

There were thick carpets on the floors, which were of a polished green stone, and the ceiling was studded with precious stones of the size, some of them, of a man's fist. There were in that ceiling pearls and rubies, diamonds and sapphires, emeralds and amethysts, and that mystic stone called lapis lazuli whose colour is a milky green, like to the blood of unicorns.

Indeed Eric had never seen nor dreamed of such a glorious place, which far outshone in its splendour of light and of colour even the palace described by Eusebius as standing on the banks of a great river called Nile – a river that flowed into the Southern Ocean. Of course, no man believed these stories of the Phoenician, given in Lord Sigurd's Hall, for it is well known that the ale horn and truth do not walk hand in hand.

The ancient man led him across a thickly carpeted floor to a table of some black wood of which the legs were carved in the shape of terrible creatures, both hoofed and winged. This table was set with a treasure hoard of dishes of precious metals encrusted with stones, and the aroma of the food which they contained made the Northman's mouth water.

'Eat,' said the old man. 'Here is better fare, I daresay,

than you have ever eaten. So have your fill of it. And be good enough while eating to answer me truthfully the questions I will put to you.'

'I will eat only if you eat also,' said Eric.

The old man made a movement of his face beneath his enormous beard which could be taken for a smile, though in such a mass of hair no smile could be seen. 'You want the Pledge of the Board,' he said, 'which is common to the Danes, Geats, Swedes, Vikings, and even the Picts, though you have no knowledge of them. Also the Saxons and Angles and Franks. I give it to you.' He reached out a scrawny arm, took the top off one of the dishes, scooped up on a finger some of the food within, and put it into his mouth. 'See – I have broken the fast with you. There is no poison here. And since I eat with you, that is your surety that I will do you no harm.'

So assured, Eric put sword and shield aside and ate with good will. He found the food to have a curious taste, sweet and aromatic, more suited to women than to men, but he ate on, for the Norsemen have this saying, 'The stay-at-home eats to satisfy his taste but the traveller to satisfy his hunger.'

While he was eating and also answering the many questions that his host put to him, a raven flew about the room. This inquisitive bird settled at last on the shoulder of the bearded man, so Eric believed that his host was under the protection of Odin, and the raven was one of the two, Hugin and Munin, who fly about the world collecting news for the god. That he should be in the presence of one of these messengers of Odin filled Eric with respect, and he noted how that raven often whispered some secret message in the ear of the old man during their talk.

Eric gave careful answer to all the questions put to him, and when he had done, his aged host remained for a long time in deep thought, the raven picking playfully at the white hairs of his beard and his head.

'Do you understand clearly why Eusebius seeks this Cup?' asked the bearded one, for they had spoken fully of this.

'Certainly, lord,' said Eric. 'It is that he fears death (for he is not one of us). So he would drink from this Cup and be assured that when he dies he will come after a little while to life again.'

'He looks for everlasting life?' asked the other.

'No. For that is something every man has,' said Eric. 'What he seeks is different. He wants never to leave this world, which he believes he will certainly achieve if he can drink from this Cup called Grail.'

At this the raven cawed, as if in mocking laughter, so it was plain that the wise bird understood all that was being said.

The old one considered this for a long time. 'What do you think of Arthur?' he asked at length.

'He is old and uncertain in his mind, in my opinion,' said Eric. 'His kingdom we found in ruins, and although it has been now restored to some order, if we were to leave this island, I believe it will be ruined again, for his people are not warriors and have not the same loyalty to him that we Northmen have to our leaders. Also, when Arthur dies, which cannot be long hence, there will be no one to take over his kingdom from him. In such cases, there is always warfare and desolation.'

'The Norsemen among you to whom he has given land will surely help to protect his kingdom.'

'My lord,' said Eric, 'it may be as you say. I will by no means oppose my wisdom, which must be very small, against yours, which is of the greatest extent. But from all the tales I have heard of such matters, the king who cannot hold his kingdom himself must soon hand it over to those whom he calls in to hold it for him. So it has often been among the Jutes and the Franks and the Geats – to make mention of only three. So it seems the kingdom of Arthur will go either to we of the Northlands or to the Angles and Saxons who will contest with us for the prize. As to who will at last rule in this island, perhaps you yourself already know.' He said this suspecting now that the old man was the god Odin in disguise.

But the old man did not give any hint as to whether he was the great god or some other, but instead spoke of matters of which Eric had no understanding. He seemed indeed to be talking at random of affairs either hidden in the past or in the future. Of what he said Eric later recalled only the following:

'The world is not the possession or the plaything of any man, for the life of the world is longer than the life of any man. Therefore a man may meddle in the affairs of the world only during his lifetime and not beyond that, when the world and all the countries in it pass to others. It is senseless then for men to seek to return from the peace of their graves to try to repossess that which has been inherited by others. It is readily to be seen that death is the means by which life progresses and the mortality of men is the greatest of all wisdoms.'

This, though spoken aloud, was said more to the raven than to Eric who, after a heavy meal, was in any case in no mood for deep talk even with a god. The old one now turned his stern gaze on the Norseman and said, 'When you next see your leader, Eusebius, who seeks the Cup, you will tell him certain things I will put into your mind while you sleep.'

'I will say whatever you command,' said Eric. 'But I do not understand anything you have said so far.'

'It is not necessary for you to understand,' replied the old man. He then rose and said to the Norseman, 'Sleep.' And though he wished greatly to ask the way to the Great Road of the West so that he might return and guide his companions, Eric the Lame fell instantly into a deep slumber at the table.

Chapter 16

When Eric was awakened by the morning rush of bird song, he found himself no longer in that splendid hall in which he had fallen asleep. The draped walls, the torches of gold, the heavily carpeted floor, and the strange table at which he had feasted and on which he had laid his head were gone. His head was now cushioned on a rock and he was lying in a little forest clearing which the white light of morning had just reached.

He jumped immediately to his feet and searched around for his weapons. They were all there. From the top of a tall pine nearby came the fluttering of wings, and a dark bird circled the clearing, gave a croak and flew off, perhaps to tell its master that Eric was now awake.

The rising sun gave the Norseman his position and he set out to the north, believing that in this direction he would find Eusebius and the rest of the party. He had gone only a few paces when he came upon the Great Road of the West, clearly laid out before him, and saw, in the trampled weeds of its surface, the marks of the passing of his own party on the previous day. Greatly encouraged, he followed this trail down the road, found where it branched to one side, leaving the main road for a side spur, and following along among the trampled ferns and thickets, had come, in an hour, to the camp of Eusebius.

'It is certain that you are under the protection of some powerful spirit,' said the redheaded Geat, Vrilig, when he saw him. 'No one expected to see you again. Here we have scarcely slept all night for fear of the Forest People.' Indeed they all looked drawn and their tempers were short from lack of rest.

'For myself,' said Eric, 'I slept well, under the protection, I believe, of the god Odin himself.' He had soon told the full story, which greatly heartened the Vikings, who now believed that Odin was undoubtedly taking an interest in their expedition.

Eric, from then on, from being among the last of that band, became now the first after Eusebius, certainly ranking as high in the esteem of his companions as Vrilig. His companions asked whether Eric had made any mention of them by name to Odin while dining with him, and whether the god had, at the mention of their names, seemed particularly interested. To all their questions Eric replied seriously and patiently and to Eusebius he gave that message the god had given him before he fell asleep, namely that the world is no man's plaything and that the mortality of men is the greatest of wisdom.

'What else did he say?' asked Eusebius after pondering this message without finding much meaning in it.

'He put me to sleep and put certain things in my mind which he said I would recall,' said Eric. 'None of these have any meaning to me, but I will repeat them to you now as they come to me. These things are as follows:

'The value of the life of a man which has been spent on his own ends is nothing, and when such a man's life is lost, nothing is lost. The value of the life of a man spent in service to others is beyond all measure. No price can be put upon it. Such a man's life is never lost. Such a man does not die.

'Also, that it is senseless for men to seek to return from their graves to try to repossess what has passed on to others. This world and all the things in it are lent to men but they do not own the world nor the things in it.

'Likewise, he said that out of darkness comes the day, that strife that ceases is but peace begun, and that that which we call time is but eternity's crippled brother. These thoughts Odin put in my mind as I slept. They are all I recall now, though others may come to me later. But do you not think it strange that so great a god should appear in so unbecoming a disguise?'

'His disguise was poor indeed if it could be penetrated by a mere mortal,' said Eusebius with a little mockery. 'It was no Odin that you visited with last night, but none other than Merlin, that wizard of Arthur's long absent from the king.'

'But he had with him a raven such as Odin has,' said Eric.

'It is no feat for a wizard to tame a raven,' said the Phoenician. 'No, it was Arthur's wizard Merlin with whom you spoke. I wish I had been there in your place, for I am sure that he and he alone knows where is this Cup, the Grail. Perhaps he has it hidden in that very cave with secret chambers in which you spent the night.'

'That cave we will never find again,' said Eric. 'When I woke this morning, it was nowhere in sight.'

'Yet we will look for it,' said the Phoenician. The sun was well up and the men now ate their breakfast, first stirring up the fire to make a thick mess of their parched oats which they carried always when journeying. Then they set out, not to find the Great Road of the West, but to seek the cave in which Eric had spent the night with the wizard.

But it fell out that no matter in which direction they searched, their search led them always to that same road which they had been unable to find on the previous night.

Plainly some enchantment was now working in the forest at the direction of the wizard. Plainly too, he had wanted to detain them during the night to question one of their number. Now it was his wish that they should be on their way out of the Forest of Eppin.

By noon then, having found nothing but the Great Road of the West, and that not once but twenty times, Eusebius abandoned his search for the cave and led the party down the road and westward. 'If Merlin wishes us to go west, then he must have some reason. It is clear however that he is not evilly disposed towards us; otherwise he could have detained us in this forest for all time.'

Now they found that road very easy to follow, and the air which they breathed was soft and fresh so that it gave them increased vigour and happiness. All were put in a good humour by the excellence of the air, and by the shining of the sun on the forest leaves, which wore the freshest of the colours of spring – some pale yellow, some pale green, and others a deeper green which promised summer. Of the trees there were pine, fir, and larch on the hilly parts where the earth was not deep, and in the valleys and dells of the forest grew the muscled oak and swelling birch and gay rowan. Here and there, high in the branches of the oaks, they could see clumps of mistletoe as big as beehives and respectfully saluted that plant which has no roots in earth or air and produces its snow-white fruit in the gloom of winter.

There was good fresh grass for their horses and sparkling streams from which man and mount could drink. Also it seemed that the sun had been stopped in the sky through some art of the wizard, for they went many miles along the road through the forest without the shafts of sunlight changing their angle through the leafy branches. Many flowers grew about their way – primrose, harebell, foxglove, and bluebells – and here and there they came in this pleasant journey upon a bush of may in full flower as though covered with deep snow. Also they were accompanied by flocks of birds – scolding magpies, yellow hammers with their shrill chatter and quick wings, and sleek blackbirds piping of fat berries and the warm sun.

Skathrig, the East Viking, after some hours of journeying through so lovely a place, spied in midafternoon in a clearing to the right of the road, a small red deer and immediately the meat hunger which can scarcely be resisted was on him. He then left the party on foot to stalk this prey, having borrowed a spear from one of the three Jutes in the party, for the East Vikings have no use for this weapon of forest dwellers.

He came upon his prey with great cunning, approaching from downwind, and having herded the deer to a clear space where there was good room for his throw, made a cast with his weapon. But the deer, by ill luck, avoided the throw and immediately the sun was gone and rain pelted down through the trees so thick that Skathrig could scarcely find his spear and get back to the road. There, after an hour of sheltering under a tree (he received little shelter from its boughs, however, for the rain came down as heavily on him as if he had been in the open) he struck out along the road. After walking another hour, he came at last on his companions, who had stopped in a dell by the roadside to rest their horses. Here the sun was shining and they were surprised to see Skathrig looking like a man plucked from the ocean.

'What befell you?' they asked. 'Did you fall into some stream?'

'You who were lucky enough to find a cave to keep dry in,' said Skathrig, 'should not mock your comrade who sought to supply you with meat for your supper.' But all said they had sought no cave and had seen no rain though they had heard both wind and rain to one side of them.

'Here is a marvel indeed,' said Skathrig, 'for until the moment I caught up with you, I have been in a tempest of rain which was worse even that that which fell the week before the death of Hjalmar the Iron Fisted.' All men knew that before the death of that great chieftain of the Jutes, the rain had fallen so heavily that many towns had been flooded and men had caught sea fish fifteen miles inland.

'Do not hunt in this forest then,' said Eusebius. 'Merlin has all things in it under his command. Truly I wish that I might meet with him, for so powerful a wizard must certainly know exactly where the Cup, Grail, is to be found.'

'It is to be found to the westward, and that is the reason he has allowed us to follow this road west,' said Vrilig. 'Nor am I sure that this Merlin has all the creatures of this forest under his enchantment. For there were last night creatures about our campfire that can scarcely be brought under the enchantment of any wizard. At the Joining of the Ring I heard myself the breathing of Formor nearby, and trembled lest that evil monster, source of all the wickedness of the world, find our camp and overwhelm us.'

'True,' said one of the Jutes, Fergus, he who had lent the spear. 'No wizard can control that Evil One whose blood is black as tar. I am certain too I heard him go by snuffing about in the dark, seeking some scent of us. Had he sight in that one eye of his which Hulises put out with a burning torch, he would certainly have seen and devoured us.'

But Eusebius laughed and said, 'At the Closing of the Ring, all men awake hear Formor,' by which he meant that at that time when night is at its darkest, just before the first lessening of the dark begins (many hours before dawn), men's minds dispose them to imagine many terrors. He quoted them a proverb of his own people, 'Courage lasts from dawn to dusk; fear from dusk to dawn.' But this saying did not sit well with the Vikings, who scorned fear (though themselves not free from that fault). They then quoted in return an Anglish saying, 'The brave man knows no night, but the night of a coward lasts a lifetime.'

It was agreed, however, that it would be best to be out of Eppin before sunset, for it was possible that the wizard Merlin might control the forest by day, but could not preserve them from Formor and from wood sprites and other foul creatures after the setting of the sun. For this reason perhaps, he was holding back the sun and for this reason too the road through the forest was scarcely travelled since the days of the Romans, who had undoubtedly built the road before those evil things had taken up their habitation in the leafy woods.

At last they found the trees thinning and as the sun rushed towards the west, they were clear of the Forest of Eppin and found the road winding before them, clearly marked, over a rolling plain, with on the northern side and some distance off a range of hills. These hills, cutting the sun's rays as it plunged west, were first golden, then of a reddish hue, and then blue and purple shadows flowed over them as evening closed around. Eusebius said that among those hills must lie the Valley of the White Horse, and that they should make an encampment where they were, for there were no dangers to be met in that countryside either by day or by night.

'The forest creatures will not venture out into this open place,' he said. 'And if we camp close to the road, we can readily see any troops of brigands or other evildoers who are travelling about.'

This was agreed. They made their camp on the top of a small hill quite close to the road and readily killed enough small game, such as rabbits and hares, to freshen their salted meat. The campfire was soon burning brightly and the men seated around on their shields with their weapons close at hand. When the ale horn was filled, Eusebius passed it first to Eric, who could without fear claim to have achieved the greatest adventure of that day, and Skathrig composed some lines concerning his visit with the wizard saying:

> Long life to that broken man on his first warfaring.
> Those who were whole have felt the bite of his sword.
> Full-limbed men have failed to batter down his shield.
> It is of Eric the Lame that I speak.
> He who ploughed behind oxen with the share
> Ploughs now redder earth with a sharper plough.
> It is said that he has already spoken with the gods.
> Certainly he has talked with one from other places
> He who has a raven for his counsellor
> And a horse of eight hoofs for his steed.
> Surely it was great-hearted Odin with whom he spoke
> Fit companion for Odin is that broken man.
> For from birth he has borne the wounds of victory over
>   a troll.

This song of praise went on for some time and was well received by all. When it was done, Eric rewarded the singer Skathrig with a boar-crested helmet given him at Arthur's feast. Watches were then set for the night and Eusebius said he would himself take the watch which included that dread time known as the Joining of the Ring.

Chapter 17

The shivering stars hung liquid in the sky when Vrilig awakened Eusebius to take his watch that night. The Bloodstar, harbinger of summer, hung low on the horizon, on the lip between sky and earth, though in the deep of the night one could not be made out from the other. Northward wheeled the Great Bear, chained to his immovable post in the sky which he was condemned by Thor to circle around for all time. Overhead moved Skata, that fast-hunting dog of the gods, but in the west a darkness told of clouds hiding all the stars from sight.

A little wind came in puffs from the northeast, cold and carrying with it a scent of marshland. Eastward the trees of the enchanted Forest of Eppin hunched against the ground under the stars, and out of the forest, before the camp, came that Great Road of the West which they were to follow.

'All is well,' said Vrilig. 'Nothing moves on earth and in the sky, only the stars. During all my watch, I have had for companion only silence. See how our companions sleep about the fire? Only you stirred in your sleep. The rest are like dead men.'

'Join them in sleep – not death,' said Eusebius. 'Who stands horse-guard now?'

'Eric the Lame,' said Vrilig. 'He sleeps beside them in that hollow out of the wind. Be sure they are safe with him, for he wakes even at the croaking of a frog. If you wish it, however, because of the dread time of the night, I will stand some part of your watch with you.'

'Sleep,' said Eusebius. 'I do not have the Norseman's fear of this hour.'

So Vrilig, putting first his shield and his sword close by him, wrapped himself in a cloak in the glow of the fire and was soon asleep. Eusebius turned to watch dark earth and dark sky (in which, however, the stars glittered in their hosts) and especially the scarcely seen track of the Great Road of the West as it led from the distant Forest of Eppin.

After a little while that bank of cloud which had been standing in the west moved eastward across the sky, spear-headed by one great tongue of vapour, and the friendly stars were extinguished one by one. Then Eusebius' eyes, more accustomed now to the dark, perceived banks of mist forming in the hollows of the land about, so that it seemed that the tops of the hills were islands floating above a death-still sea. The mist rose higher, the islands were gone, and gone too was all the earth. The Phoenician, though he stood just beyond the circle of the fire, could see neither its glow nor the forms of his sleeping companions in the silver flood of the ground mist.

Stouthearted, he took from its case that special weapon which he alone loved, and also some of the arrows which he could speed from it with such deadly skill. These arrows he put into the ground at his feet, the points buried in the earth, the shafts close to his hand lest he have need for them in a hurry. Such is the habit of the users of these weapons to speed up their work.

Now that mist which had drowned first the valleys and then the hilltops thickened, and that little wind which had blown fitfully at the start of the watch increased in strength. Its puffs became gusts which sped the mist in cold clouds of strange shape past Eusebius and over the sleeping camp behind him.

Then, from that same mist, he heard first grunts and screams and coughs, and such noises as might be made by a vast herd of animals on the move down the road towards him. Then out of the mist came a host of stooped dwarfs, naked and covered with hair, their small unbearded heads thrust forward from their big chests, their teeth bared. They carried in their hands clubs, some of wood and some made of the leg bones of their own kind. Others among them carried corpses on their backs – corpses of their own kind, some full-grown and some children. Others carried the carcasses of small deer or of sheep – and those of their own kind and those of animal kind they bore in the same fashion as if both were food. Then Eusebius, not sure whether he dreamed it or not, knew that these were the Anthropophagi, the Eaters of Men, known by all to live in the wild places of the earth.

This foul horde came in a swarm down that Great Road before the camp, not plainly seen but thrusting into view from the folds of the mist. At times he saw but a head or a shoulder or a foot, and at times several of these horrors grinned before him, baring their dog teeth with which they could tear the flesh from his body.

He would certainly have sunk to the ground and hidden behind his shield if able. But some power held him upright, and he was compelled to stand then in full view of this multitude of horrible things as they trooped past him, howling, screeching, and barking as they went. There was with them a smell foul and rancid which made the air repugnant to breathe. This smell seemed to come as much from the bodies of these Eaters of Men as from their breath. But though many looked at him from eyes buried in the depths of their skulls, none harmed him or moved towards him. The fear he felt of them, however, went beyond fear of harm to his body only. He feared that they might, if they caught true sight of him, enslave his spirit and make him into one of them – an eater of his own kind.

In a while, however, they were gone, the gusting wind was stilled, the mist thinned, and with his limbs released from the grasp of fear, Eusebius was able to run to the camp to give the alarm to his sleeping comrades. But though he shook many of them hard and raised a great clamour, yet none, not even Knute, would awaken. He was about to seek out Eric the Lame, that lightest of sleepers who was guarding the horses, when once again the air thickened, the wind gusted and whirled the clouds of mist about him – now silver and now dark – and once again there came to his ears from the direction of the enchanted Forest of Eppin a tumultuous sound.

Now the sound was of cries more humanlike – shouts of men and shrieks of women, all in terror or in pain. These cries filled him also with fear and he beheld rushing down the road towards him, now seen plainly and now obscured by the mist, boys and girls, all wounded and bloodied, and riding among them, running them to earth, striking at them with swords and clubs, mounted men clad in armour. Without pity they struck at the helpless fugitives. Those they brought to the ground they rode over with their horses and trampled. Those who stopped to help the fallen were likewise ridden down and trampled. This slaughter of the helpless surrounded the Phoenician and he struck about him at those merciless horsemen with his sword. But they neither saw nor felt him, having no more substance than the mist itself.

Then this carnage ceased and the air was again quiet. The mist thinned. The hidden hills returned to view and the valleys between them. Even the stars came out once more in the sky and Eusebius, bathed in sweat despite the cold of the night, tried again in vain to awaken his companions. He shouted to them and shook them roughly, but they were like the dead about the campfire.

Nor could he even rouse Eric the Lame, who sat by his shield in the hollow where the horses were hobbled. Among his own companions Eusebius was yet alone and the Joining of the Ring had yet another hour to go.

Nor was it long before the next terror presented itself. This time there was no mist, no wind, and no sound. But out of the dark shape of the forest there came a flood of flames leaping upward towards the sky – yellow, red, and in places boiling with acrid smoke. Nearer and nearer came these fires, breaking out on all sides of the watcher.

Some of the flames were a hundred feet over his head. Yet he could not move a foot. Through these gigantic fires he now saw men and women running, their black mouths opened in silent screams of torment. Hither and thither they went in excruciating agony, their limbs on fire, burning but never burned. At first there were but a handful of these miserable creatures, and then a hundred and then a thousand and then thousands beyond all counting. Then as with all things that had appeared previously, the flames died away, the tortured disappeared, and there was left only the blackness of the night below and above the pitiless stars.

Sweating with fear, Eusebius awaited the next ordeal. That he had survived the first three gave him no comfort, for he felt that he was being preserved to be destroyed after further terrors, and what had been shown to him so far was then but the foretaste of what he would have to endure when his own time for destruction had come.

In vain he tried again to awaken his companions. They were gone from him in that borderland called sleep, which lies between this world and the place beyond. Nor could he summon them back. And now he had more need of them than ever, for again that cloud with its forked tongue spread from west to east; again the stars were one by one extinguished in the sky and that mist of dread arose to drown first the valley and then the hills.

Again the Phoenician felt the fitful wind blow in gusts around him, and out of the mist from the direction of the forest came clamour as of birds or bats chirping, shrilling, and twittering, the noise increasing with every instant. With these two, overpowering the wind itself, came a noisome smell of carrion and then in the dark folds and opening of the mist Eusebius saw coming towards him and snuffing about like questing hounds all the dishonoured dead of the world. Some were warriors in armour who had fled the field of battle. Now rotted in their war gear, they groped with yellow bones along the ground, seeking that one man alive and awake – Eusebius himself. Others were murderers, brigands, thieves, all clad in the clothing of their unnamed graves, casting here and there and making their birdlike chirps while they searched for the Phoenician.

Now he dared not shout for succour lest he attract these seekers. Sword he knew was useless against the dead, nor could any degree of courage prevail against those who are beyond all hurt. He did not quail and run but took sword and shield, though these could do him no service, for he was still determined to lay about him rather than to submit to these grave dwellers like the rabbit to the wolf.

Nearer and nearer they came, for it seemed they could find what was alive, and their clamour of cheeps and twitters rose. Then the wind blowing strongly from him to them, they knew plainly where he was and rushed down upon him. Now the Phoenician, surrounded by the gibbering swarm, struck about him valiantly with sword, but though he lopped off arm, leg, and head, these but joined again to their owner, who reached out to get at him. Then above this throng of ghouls rose one twice as big as any. He was clad in corselet of mail and helmet of iron, crested with horsehair. His flesh was all but gone from his face and he reached with deathly hands for the Phoenician to quench in him that life which all envied. Certainly there was no hope for Eusebius had he not bethought himself of that ring with the red stone which Arthur had given him at his setting out.

Quickly he took that ring off his thumb and held it up in the face of the ogre who sought to destroy him. And in a moment, with a screech of despair, all that foul multitude had gone. Gone also was the mist and the grave stench. The gusty wind died away and was replaced by a gentle breeze which carried with it the sweet scent of summer hay. The stars reappeared once more in the sky, and turning, Eusebius saw coming towards him Skathrig, son of the priestess of Odin.

'The Closing of the Ring is over,' he said. 'It is now my turn to watch. How went things with you in that foul time?' He looked earnestly in the pale face of the Phoenician. But Eusebius, not wishing to dismay his men, made an evasive reply and turned away from him.

Chapter 18

The following day started with a rainstorm, the wind sweeping in from the west and carrying with it a host of lowering clouds whose sagging bellies swept the low hills as they went by. All were drenched, for in the open rolling landscape no shelter could be found. The men of Eusebius' party moved in this hiss of the downpour westward until they came to a place where there was a shallow hollow and on one side a few overhanging rocks of white chalk. Under these they took shelter, but their horses had to content themselves with turning their backs to the storm and enduring the weight of the rain.

Eusebius was deep in thought about the significance of those terrors to which he had been exposed during the night. He was sure that there was some hidden meaning to them, associated perhaps with the messages Merlin had sent him through Eric the Lame, but whatever that meaning was, it escaped him at present. By sly questions he tried to discover from Eric the Lame whether he had heard or seen anything during the time of the Closing of the Ring. But he said that nothing had disturbed him during his watch though he had had, sleeping among the horses, uneasy dreams of which he could recall little.

'It seems to me,' he told Eusebius, 'that you were in danger and calling for help. Yet no man could get to you. I cannot say how this was. I remember only that you needed aid but could not be helped. Were you indeed in danger?'

'There is always danger on such a journey as this,' replied Eusebius. 'This rain seems strange to me. Who would expect so heavy a deluge now that winter is past?'

'Do you think that it is perhaps the result of some spell?' asked Eric.

'It delays us as the loss of the road through the Forest of Eppin delayed us. If there is some creature trying to stop us getting to Avalon where I must find this Cup, then we should press on despite the storm.'

A consultation was then held and it was agreed to continue despite the fury of the wind and the rain, for certainly they could not remain that night in the flooded hollow below the shelter of those miserable rocks. Off they set again, hunched over the horses which themselves walked with heads low to avoid the sting of the rain. The wind howled and moaned about them. The rain came in white clouds whirling through the dark air, sometimes almost level with the ground. It seemed that the rage of the tempest increased after they had decided to defy it. Their horses stumbled in the liquid mud which covered the Great Road of the West, and the whole landscape (what could be seen of it) seemed now alive, for the grasses and bushes and other rank growths both on the road and to the side of it waved and writhed like reptiles beneath their horse's hoofs. The horsemen, with bent heads, rode behind the shelter of their shields, and the horses often staggered in the vicious gusts of wind.

The road now led over a series of low hills and it was not long before the valleys between them were flooded with muddy rivers whipped white by rain and wind. Through these swift-flowing torrents the horsemen struggled, never sure of the depth before them. Now indeed all would have been glad to find some shelter again, and many were sorry that they had left those pitiful rocks which had at least given them protection from the worst of the wind. But no refuge lay at hand and no man spoke of going back. So they went on, dismounting to struggle ahead of their horses through the worst of the torrents.

At last they came to higher ground, indeed to the flanks of a number of larger hills through which the Great Road of the West turned to the south. Here they had some shelter from the wind in the lee of the hills and though they had to leave the road – which had become a river – their horses found a more trustworthy footing. By the middle of the afternoon the storm began to abate. The clouds parted and the sun came out, and as the wind dropped the drenched landscape glittered with wet light and horse and rider were soon steaming as they dried off.

Still there was not enough of the day left for much further travel. They had covered only twelve miles at most and their steeds were tired. Just before sunset they came to an old cave high up on the hillside and here made their camp. There was room in the cave for men and horses and they soon had a fire going and were able to get dry. Eusebius would have very much preferred to be farther from the Forest of Eppin and dreaded the onset of the night. He again took the watch at the Closing of the Ring, but nothing untoward happened, and the next day the sun shone brightly and it was hard indeed to believe that so furious a storm had beset them only the day before.

So they made their way westward, passing through the Valley of the White Horse, so named because on the side of an immense hill was a figure of a white horse made in the ground by the removal of the grass to the chalk below. This magnificent beast would have made a fine steed for Odin except that it had but four legs whereas Odin's favourite had eight.

From there they passed through that Great Plain of the

Stones of which Arthur had warned Eusebius. They made sure (following the king's warning) to cross this in daylight. And yet they were nearly trapped on it by the approach of dusk.

They had come to the plain shortly after dawn on the third day of their journey. On the horizon of that vast level area (interrupted by not a single hill or valley) they could see the Great Stones. These stones, as they came nearer, were found to be arranged in groups of three, each group being composed of two upright stones and one stone across the top of them. These groups of three were arranged in a circle, and the stones were so enormous that it was impossible for them to have been erected by ordinary mortals. That they were the work of giants was beyond all doubt, and it seemed possible that the same giants who had put up this mighty ring of stones might also have carved on the hillside that vast figure of a horse. This was no comfortable thought for the Norsemen, the struggle of the gods against the giants being well known to them.

The Great Road of the West passed within a mile of the Stone Circle, but not a man left the road to look at this curiosity. Rather they hurried by and then they found that fast as they had come upon the stones, they seemed incapable of leaving them behind. Though they galloped their horses, lashing them with their naked swords, they seemed to get only a slight distance away from the foreboding Stone Circle, which must be left behind by dark.

Vrilig, with the cunning which has so often been the saving of the Geats, found, however, a way to defeat the power of the stones.

'When we were approaching them we came on very fast,' he said. 'But now that we go away, we labour as hard as we can and can scarcely make half a mile in an hour. Let every man dismount then, and face the stones as if he were walking towards them. But let him walk backwards and perhaps with this strategy the stones will be deceived.'

This advice was followed immediately and proved entirely successful. For from the time they got off their horses and, facing the stones, walked backwards from them, they went at a rapid rate. So it was that as the sun reached the end of its journey for that day, they came at last to the edge of the Great Plain and could make camp for the night far from the forest of Eppin and out of sight of the evil stonecraft of the giants.

Chapter 19

The place to which the Vikings had now come was marked on the chart as the Singing Hills. Of this they had been warned by Arthur that it was inhabited by a race of dwarfs both malevolent and treacherous. But in the first day of journeying through these hills, which extended like the waves of the sea from horizon to horizon, and seemed – also like the waves – to have no ending, the Norsemen met no dwarfs nor could they discover why these hills should bear their strange name.

However, on the second day about midmorning they heard snatches of some chant on the north side of them. This sound was so faint that for a time they could not be sure that they indeed heard anything. They thought they might be deceived by their imaginations, overstretched for the sound of song. Whenever they stopped to catch this chanting more clearly above the rumble of their horses' hoofs, it died away and all that was to be heard was the seething of the wind, rising and falling over the glittering grasslands.

Towards noon, still continuing their way along the Great Road of the West, the singing became louder and clearer were some of the words of the song being sung to them – words which had no meaning for the Vikings, being in that alien tongue familiar only to dwarfs. The words went as follows, as closely as could be recorded:

Iasacht imim iseal ithim labhairt
Mairteol maithim miam obhairt
Radharc raithe rumbar sceartairt
Go bra go bra go bra ireanne.

There were of course many other words to the song, which was plainly a song of marching. But these made a chorus repeatedly sung and with great force. Nearer and nearer came the sound of the song, but still no sign could be seen of the singers. The Vikings rode to the top of a hill to oversee the countryside as far as they could for the marching singers but caught not a glimpse of them – not as much as the sight of a banner or the tip of a spear held aloft.

'Not only are they dwarfs,' said Eusebius, 'but they are invisible.'

'They must be mounted,' said Vrilig, unsheathing his great sword with a grin. 'They come on too fast to be on foot. However, we will do our best against them. Surely they are flesh and bone, for spirits do not go about under the sun. I am glad that this day, which has been dull so far, promises to now provide some sport.'

'We will without a doubt be surrounded here in the open,' said Eric the Lame. 'While I am still new to battle-craft, I would suggest that we try to form a shield wall at the top of this hill so as to be able to meet them on all sides.'

This was done, the men arranging themselves in a circle on the crest of the hill, shields together but with sufficient room over the top of them to give play for war hammer, axe and singing sword, each according to the fancy of the warrior. Eusebius, however, stood alone on the crest of the hill with that weapon of his which he much loved, but which the Vikings regarded as one dishonourable to use since it permitted a man to kill his foe from some distance away.

The sound of the Marching Song of the Dwarfs was soon so loud that the Vikings had themselves to shout to be heard above the singing. Furthermore, the sound which had come orginally from the north now extended to west, east, south, and in between so they were without doubt surrounded by dwarfs and yet could not see any of them. Some feared that these were not mortal foes but spirits put under some deceiving enchantment wrought by that bearded figure whom Eric the Lame had met in the deeps of the Forest of Eppin.

There was much uncertainty then among the party of Eusebius and many of the warriors produced the charms they had obtained – often at great sacrifice – to ward off such dangers. Some had bundles of dried claws of the golden eagle, others the skull and beak of the sea eagle, others the feet of rabbits, the teeth of bears, the feathers of ravens, or medals scribed with the Crooked Cross of Odin. None who had these things were ashamed to produce them, and like good comrades allowed those who had made no such wise preparation for travel abroad to handle their charms for a moment so as to receive some portion of their protection.

From the top of the hill at which the Vikings had taken up their stand (with the horses in the centre of their circle) they could see a number of other hills around with folds and valleys between them, which, interlinking with each other, joined the valley which circled the hill on which they stood. Now from all these hills, or rather from the valleys between them, came the sound of this song. Louder and louder and from all sides it came, and still no one was to be seen. And then with the suddenness of a thunder clap (but with the opposite effect) the song ceased.

Not a note was to be heard and the sky no longer

seemed to quiver from the singing of thousands of voices. Once again could be heard the hiss of the wind through the grass and the jingle of harness from the horses or the dull clump of their feet when they moved. Then suddenly it seemed that the sky rained stones. Thousands of stones, the size of wild plums, hurtled down upon the Vikings, rattling off their helmets, drawing blood when they hit naked arm or exposed face. This deluge fell on the horses equally with the men. These panicked in fright and in pain. Rearing up, they lashed out with their hoofs, broke through the Viking ring, and half of them thundered away down the hill whinnying with fear.

This storm of stones, which left those missiles thick upon the ground of the hilltop, lasted but a few seconds. But some of the men were hurt, and had the surprising hail of stones continued for some minutes, despite their helmets and shields, a great number of them would have been heavily wounded or even killed.

When the stone storm ceased, from one of the valleys between the folds of the hills came a horseman accompanied by about twenty followers – all of them dwarfs and mounted on horses hardly any bigger than hunting dogs. Their leader, who rode a little ahead and was armoured in a shirt of ring mail that reached to his ankles, was smaller rather than larger than his followers. He carried a tiny battle axe fastened to his wrist by a leather thong. He had a nose as fierce and hooked as the beak of a hawk, and from under a curious helmet, which came to a point like a cone, tumbled a fall of hair as black as a raven's feathers. His beard was cut off square a little above the centre of his chest, and hanging on his chest, outside of his shirt of mail, was some kind of amulet or charm in the form of a medal of large size set with precious stones that flashed in the sun.

This manikin with his followers rode halfway up the hill towards the Norsemen, and Vrilig chuckled grimly and said to he who stood beside him, 'If he will but come on within reach of my sword, I will be able to boast that with one blow I cut man and horse in two.'

'There is a saying in my country which is very wise, that the oliphant, which is the biggest creature on earth, is often destroyed by ants,' said Eusebius. 'Therefore let no one offer this manikin any harm unless we are attacked. I myself will go forward and talk to him.'

'Nay, my lord,' cried Eric. 'Let me go. Surely it is only fitting that half a man be met by half a man?' For the Lame One still looked for glory at every opportunity.

'That may be true,' said Eusebius, frowning at the laughter of the Norsemen (for whatever the danger, they loved a pointed jest). 'But it is also fitting that a chief should talk with a chief. Therefore I will go. Also I speak many tongues and may be able to find one common to both of us.'

So he pushed his way through the shield wall, carrying neither sword nor shield, and walked in that many-coloured coat of his down to the mounted dwarf. 'Venimus in pace; pax tecum,' he said, using the Roman tongue to tell the dwarf that they came in peace and wished peace to him and his followers. To his surprise, the dwarf, who even mounted did not quite reach head to head with him, replied in the dialect of the language of the Norsemen which Arthur and his followers used and which he could understand without great difficulty.

'You come armed,' the dwarf said. 'Who are you and where are you bound and what brings you armed into our hills?'

'I am Eusebius from the land of Phoenicia. I lead this band of Vikings and we seek the Cup of Life called Grail,

137

which is to be found on the island of Avalon. I am friend to King Arthur of the Brythons and we have used our swords only to restore his authority over his kingdom. And who are you and who are your people?'

'I am Gro Me'ak, King of the Small Men, called Firbolg,' replied the dwarf. 'We are the oldest people in this land, older than Arthur and his people. Older even than the Picts or the Cymri. Before any men came to this land we were here. You may not pass through the hills unless I give you permission. You are our prisoners. So tell your men to lay down their weapons.'

Eusebius shook his head. 'That they will never do. Men such as these would sooner be dead than lay aside their weapons on the orders of another. But there need be no bloodshed between us. We come in peace, as I have said.'

'That you came at all is a warlike act,' said Gro Me'ak. 'You were not invited here.' He raised a tiny silver horn to his mouth, no bigger than the plaything of a child, and blew three such small blasts on it that the Vikings on the hill laughed aloud at so small a summons. Immediately from every valley and fold of the hills surrounding them came a tide of these Men of the Firbolg, not scores or hundreds but thousands of them, all armoured and mounted and carrying weapons of many kinds, though each of them had a sling and a bag of stones.

'Tell your men to lay aside their weapons,' repeated Gro Me'ak when this host had entirely surrounded the Vikings.

'That, as I have explained, I cannot do, for I will not be obeyed,' said Eusebius. 'No Norseman would obey so dishonourable a command. Why do you insist on this matter? Surely you are numerous enough to kill us all if you wish, and it cannot be said that so small a band as mine can pose any menace to so large a host as yours.

Prudence alone would forbid us attacking you and, as I have said, all we wish to do is pass through your country on the Great Road of the West. If you wish I will, however, hand over to you my own sword as a sign that we plan no harm to you or your people.'

He then offered his sword, hilt first, to Gro Me'ak, who took it with some difficulty. In fact, although the sword of Eusebius was small, the King of the Firbolg was but a foot taller than the blade. Nonetheless, Gro Me'ak managed to get the sword on his shoulder, where it projected like a spear, and a rumble of applause went up from the host of his followers.

'Bid your men sheathe their weapons and come with us,' said Gro Me'ak. 'No hurt will be done to them if they obey, and do not resist or attack us treacherously as the Romani often did until we taught them better manners.'

'Let me explain this matter to them,' said Eusebius, and walked back up the hill to his band. There he told the Norsemen what was demanded of them by the King of the Firbolg. It was not easy for such warriors to do the bidding of dwarfs. Indeed, the fathers of many of them had gone joyfully to their red beds of death similarly outnumbered, but by men of their own size. None then were prepared to sheathe their swords at the orders of the king of these small people, and all the wiles of the Phoenician were required to make them do so.

'Surely,' he said, 'you do not want it said that you wreaked havoc with your weapons among an army of children? Is that the boast you wish to make in the hall of Lord Sigurd when you return to your homes – that with sword and battle-axe you cut a swath among men no bigger than boys? Come, I am sure that you hold your weapon-honour higher than that.'

With such words of guile did the Phoenician cajole his

unruly followers into sheathing their weapons and permitting themselves to be led away by the Firbolg. They then went off to the northward in a sea of the Firbolg which now (no concealment being needed) flooded over hill and valley, a dark mass of tiny men and tiny horses among whom the Norsemen were true giants.

Amazing it was for Geat, Swede, Finn, and Dane to see these toy warriors, grizzled and bearded, conducting themselves entirely like full-grown and battle-hardened men. Streams through which the Vikings splashed, with the water up to the bellies of their steeds, were roaring torrents capable of drowning man and beast of the Firbolg. Yet they plunged into them without hesitating, whacking their terrified mounts on their streaming flanks with the flat of their swords, urging them on, and never showing the slightest fear. But they were surly and distrustful of the Vikings and would talk little to them.

They continued northward for half a day, the hills all the time getting higher, and at last, with the approach of evening, came to a hilly countryside covered with low shrubs. Here, to the surprise of the Norsemen, they found themselves travelling along a very well-made road, not overgrown like the Great Road of the West, but excellently maintained. This road was wide enough for six of the Firbolg to ride abreast and led towards a purpling mountain still to the northward. They could see the road, white against the green of the hills and the shrubs, climb the lower part of this purple mountain and then disappear in its side.

'Surely the road does not go through the mountain,' Eusebius asked of the dwarf king.

'It goes into the mountain as you can plainly see,' said Gro Me'ak. 'And our city is inside the heart of that place. We live below the ground, and let me warn you that this place to which you are being taken is but one of the dwelling places of the Firbolg. They are to be found through this whole country, and it being the pastime of our people to sing a great deal in their homes, for this reason this countryside is known among the Celts and Cymri and Brythons as the Singing Hills.'

'And have you always been a folk that lived under the earth?' asked Eusebius, who was forever seeking information about others.

'No,' replied Gro Me'ak. 'Before the first of the invaders came to this island, many thousands of years ago, we lived above the ground and thought ourselves the only people in the world. But we learned that it was easy for a bigger foe to destroy the cities of people of our size. We had always known of these caverns under the hills hereabouts and had used them as storehouses for food. Milk will keep fresh a week in these caverns, which are cool, and butter has never been known to turn sour, such is the purity of the air. We took to living in these caves ourselves in the First Wars, and so were safe from the first invaders and from all who have followed, with whom, however, we have many times been in battle.

'Now we think it is foolish for men to live on the surface of the earth, exposed to every whim of the weather, when it is possible to live below the earth and be exposed neither to snow nor sleet, to rain nor fog, wind nor heat.'

'It is a marvel to me indeed that there should be room underground for so vast a throng,' said Eusebius.

'There is more room below the ground than above it,' said Gro Me'ak. 'For on the surface there is but one level, while below ground there are many.'

'But what of light?' asked Eusebius. 'Thousands of torches, burning day and night, would scarcely suffice to give light for the dwelling of so many people. And surely, even below the ground, the heat and smoke from those torches would be beyond bearing.'

'All these matters have been well attended to as you shall see,' said Gro Me'ak. 'I think you will find that when you have spent a few days with us, you will not be so ready to return to living on the surface of the world – at the mercy of the blinding light, the descending rain, and every wind that blows.'

The road of the Firbolg, along which that vast army now travelled, came at last to the entrance in the flank of the mountain which led to their dwelling place. But this entrance was not open to be used by anyone who came across it. Indeed, Eusebius could see no entrance at all, but only a road which ceased suddenly before the face of a glistening black rock, which was not smoothed like a door, but full of knobs and crevices, rounds and hollows, as are all rock cliffs by nature.

The Vikings were at the head of the column with Gro Me'ak and his bodyguard, and all stopped thirty paces away from this stern cliff on which Eusebius noted with his keen eyes no moss grew, though to the side there were mosses and lichens on the rocks.

'Who shall open the door?' cried Gro Me'ak. 'Let it be a sure hand, since strangers watch.'

'I,' said one of the companions of this tiny king.

'Aim well then, Drogith. Let stone speak straight to stone,' said Gro Me'ak.

Drogith, who had the beak nose and shallow face of all the Firbolg, selected a stone from his bag, fitted it in his sling, and with a grin at Vrilig, who had not refrained entirely from boasting of his prowess with the sword, whirled the sling over his head and cast the stone loose. Up it whirled like a lark in spring until almost out of sight, then making a beautiful turn in the air, came down again to strike the upper surface of a knob of rock on the top of the cliff. Immediately the whole rock face before them commenced sinking slowly into the ground.

'What say you to that, Big One?' asked Drogith of Vrilig. 'Is it not true that while you whirled your sword for the deathblow, I could, from far off, have put a stone through your throat?'

'Even the boys in my homeland, who are no bigger than you, do not fight each other in so dishonourable a manner,' said Vrilig.

'Who wins the fight tells the story and has the honour,' said Drogith. 'You must get off your horse to enter or you will crush that big head of yours.' Truly the entrance to the dwelling of the Firbolg, while it would permit a man of normal height to pass on foot, was not high enough for a mounted man.

So all the Vikings had to dismount, though the Firbolg remained seated on their small but sturdy steeds. In they went, first through a cool and dim tunnel in which the light for a while diminished so that it was possible for Eusebius to see only those immediately near to him. Then, however, the light increased, and that clamour of their passing (echoing back from wall and ceiling of rock around them) diminished and died away to a few muffled thumps and clinks.

Underfoot the ground was soft and moist but not slippery. Though he could not see the ground, Eusebius felt that he walked over a carpet of moss or perhaps of fallen leaves. Darkness was replaced by greyness, and greyness by a pearly light, tinged with a mild pink, very pleasant to the eyes and seeming to be soft even to the touch.

The vexations, irritations, and concerns of the Vikings (forced to do the bidding of a host of manikins) left them. They felt that glow of warmth and of kindness which overcomes all but the surliest of men when seated at the ale feast of their lord on a winter night, with the firelight playing cheerily on walls and rafters. Now it was possible to see about and hard to believe that they were in a cavern. They found about them a strange and lovely countryside with a roadway of soft earth or mould under their feet, and on either side and ahead, rolling fields of mushrooms, some white as bone, some yellow, some purple, some pink, and looking like hosts of flowers carpeting the ground.

'It seems that we dream or are enchanted,' said Eric, walking close to Eusebius and talking to him over the head of Gro Me'ak's little horse. 'We will awaken to the roaring rain and the wind.'

'You do not dream,' said the King of the Firbolg. 'Nor have you yet seen the beginning of our kingdom under the earth. Tell me, do you feel angry with any man?'

'Not in any degree,' said Eric. 'All are friends and I am friend to all.'

Then Gro Me'ak grinned and said, 'Give your sword to the horseman by you, for certainly you will not need to use it among your friends.'

Eric was about to unhitch his sword belt and surrender his weapon when Eusebius stopped him. 'By the same token,' said the sly Phoenician, 'there is no need to take away the sword of one who is a friend of yours. Only foes watch each other's blades, so let Eric the Lame keep his sword and my other men keep theirs also.'

He glanced around and was dismayed to find that several of the Vikings, including Knute, had parted with their swords or were parting with them, under the influence of that pleasant air, to the Firbolg. So he sent Vrilig back among them to say that they must get possession of their weapons again. Yet he found it hard to keep a sense of suspicion in this mild warm air and pleasant light.

The road went gently downwards for a considerable distance, but not in a steady slope. At times indeed it rose slightly and at others curved to the right or the left, but mostly to the right. Eusebius, whose mind was never lulled, was aware that they were going down in an enormous spiral of perhaps a mile in diameter, into the very roots of the mountain which they had entered. Yet the light remained the same and indeed seemed to become brighter. This light he could now see came from vast globes suspended overhead, but whether they were suspended in midair or against the rock ceiling of the vast cavern he could not decide. All beyond the lights and between these lights was dark.

Now the countryside changed. No longer were there only mushrooms in the field, but watermelons and tasselled corn, growing enormously high, and here and there were pretty woods and copses of birch and elder, hazelnut and willow. Indeed there were streams and lakes, and now houses here and there, and out of these came more of the Firbolg – men, women, and children – to watch the return of this enormous army and look with amazement on the giant Vikings and the giant horses which had been captured.

At last, when they had by the reckoning of the Phoenician gone a full mile deep into the earth, the road straightened out and broadened. The surface changed from earth to stone, and ahead of them they could see a castle, heavily walled about, with a fast-flowing stream circling it, and huge towers on the four corners of the wall. Within these walls, the castle itself reared upward, carved out of the rock of the mountain.

They had soon crossed the drawbridge over the castle moat and then over a courtyard of cobblestones and up some broad stone stairs to a terrace over the door of the castle itself. The door was of oak, heavily studded with iron and six feet tall – a tremendous height for the Firbolg but little to the Vikings. Within, they found themselves in a Great Hall, with benches about and three fireplaces, one at each end and one in the middle of the long inner wall of the hall. This wall was hung with weapons, the greater number of them captured from the enemies of the Firbolg. Among these weapons (silent witnesses of old battles and heroes once famed and now forgotten) were many of the swords of the Romani and also their four-sided curved shields, as well as many lances twenty feet long, and battle maces and coats of chain armour and suits of plate armour.

There were saddles for horses of full size – not the small steeds of the Firbolg – and gauntlets, and all these things, hanging mutely on the walls, seemed to Eusebius (less affected than his companions by the soothing light and air of this underground country), to spell danger for his band. Still, he affected good humour and trust. Gro Me'ak led them from the Great Hall into a dining hall of equal size, where they were served with excellent dishes of wild boar and the venison of red deer, hedgehog stews, dishes of turbot and lampreys and pigeon pies and meat pasties of many kinds, though rather more highly spiced than suited the Vikings.

The Norsemen, lulled by the charm of the light and the pleasant mood of their captors (whom they now thought of as friends and hosts), seemed to have lost all their manly reserve. Vrilig, whose greatest joy was to wield his sword in battle, had forgotten all the delights of the fray and had his arm around the shoulders of one of the Firbolg and pledged him eternal friendship with a cup of black mushroom wine which was liberally served to them.

Eric the Lame, by nature and upbringing silent and

inclined to suspicion, related openly and smilingly their adventures since leaving their homeland, and their plans for the future. Even Skathrig, who since his mother had been a priestess of Odin had some power to see into the minds of others, was singing, like one slightly in his cups, with the harpists who had been brought in for their entertainment. That he did not know either the tune or the words did not deter him, for the grim Viking sang as a child does – out of pleasure in music and not knowledge of music.

It was clear to Eusebius that none of this was natural. It was not natural for his men to have become like children at play. It was not natural, having been captured by the Firbolg, to be feasted in such a manner, and his astute brain told him that it was not natural either that so vast an army should have gone forth to capture so small a band as his. Therefore he concluded that the Firbolg had sent out for some other prey, but coming upon him and his Vikings had decided that these were a sufficient result for the time being. Their first purpose in setting out was, perhaps, still unachieved.

Eusebius therefore questioned Gro Me'ak about this saying, 'It seems to me, my Lord Gro Me'ak, that you set nets for whales but caught only mackerel. You will never convince me that you led out five thousand men to capture only fifty, even though twice your size.'

Gro Me'ak, his hawknose in golden goblet of black mushroom wine which had a woodsy bouquet not unlike that golden wine of Lusitania which is called Sheriz, cocked a bushy eye at the Phoenician over the rim of the goblet and then, having drunk, wiped his thin lips with the back of his hand.

'It is true,' he said, 'that one hundred of my stone throwers could have captured your whole band. We had known of your coming many days. We of the Firbolg, as I have hinted to you, were once lords of the whole of the White Island. Though now we rule in only a small part, yet we still regard the whole land as our heritage. Be sure then that we had our spies out to look for you and knew of your coming.'

'And then set upon us with all your army?' asked Eusebius, for this point puzzled him.

'I see your mind is scarcely affected by our hospitality,' said Gro Me'ak. 'You still think as if you were on the windy surface above us. Very well, I will be honest with you. My spies tell me that there is a great host of the people called Saxons two days' march to the south. They come as the next invaders of this island, already so many times invaded.

'When I heard of your party coming down the Great Road of the West, I suspected you might be part of the Saxon invasion. We set out to intercept you and also to meet with that other invasion of Saxons. But when we saw what manner of men you were, not of the Saxons at all, but claiming to be friends of Arthur and dressed differently, it was time to take council once more and so we brought you back here. But that army which you saw and which accompanied us back to the entrance to our underground land is again on its way to meet the Saxon hosts. We will soon have news of how they have fared. But have some more of our mushroom wine, which will help you digest the big meal you have eaten and is more nourishing than any drink on earth or beneath.'

He filled the Phoenician's goblet and replenished his own. Then he toasted Eusebius and drank deeply, but the Phoenician only sipped the liquid.

'What do you plan to do with us now?' asked Eusebius.

'No harm if your story is true,' said Gro Me'ak. 'If,

however, you have lied to me, and you are really the advance guard of a further war party of your own folk coming down the Great Road of the West, then you will be stripped of your armour and stoned to death by my slingers.'

'If my story proves true, as indeed it is,' said the Phoenician, 'are we then to be allowed to go free?'

But to this Gro Me'ak did not reply directly, merely repeating that no harm would come to them.

That night they were led to different quarters to sleep, though Eusebius protested against this breaking up of his band. But in his protests he got no support from his men, who were now as amiable as puppies. His warriors told him to put aside his foolish fears and suspicions and to remember that they were guests of the Firbolg and had eaten with them. Therefore the ancient laws of hospitality, respected in every part of the world, guaranteed that no harm would come to them. Furthermore, the Vikings said, smiling happily, the Firbolg were like brothers to them and would never raise a hand to hurt them but had promised (so they said) to aid them in any way they could. So they chafed at Eusebius for his suspicions and said that he was indeed a stranger and did not possess the generous and open heart of the people of the North.

'When a fly lands on your horse's nose, you look about to see who sent it,' they said. 'Be easy now among your friends and enjoy the pleasant moments which are so few in the lives of warriors.'

But Eusebius would not forget his suspicions and was angered to see that most of his men had parted with their weapons to the Firbolg. Even the three Jutes had relinquished their spears, though the saying 'The Jute is married to his spear' is known throughout the world.

Making a weapon count as well as he could, he found

only ten of his men still armed – that is to say, three Danes, four Swedes, one of the North Vikings, Vrilig the Geat, and himself. But then he found that Skathrig still retained his great double-bitted axe, though he sang still a tuneless little chant in memory of the harpists and smiled on all around.

Eusebius managed to get Vrilig and Skathrig as sleeping companions and noted the corridors down which the others of his band trooped to their own quarters. The dormitory was of no great size and had three beds in it, but being built for the Firbolg, they were too small by far for the Vikings. These then settled down on the floor and were soon asleep, despite the light which glowed soft and pearly pink in the ceiling above.

No guard was set on their door, a circumstance which also aroused the suspicions of the Phoenician, for he reasoned that they were certainly prisoners, that Gro Me'ak knew that Eusebius was uneasy and would certainly attempt to escape if the opportunity offered.

'Perhaps,' said the Phoenician to himself, 'he thinks that with my companions unarmed, I would not desert them here below the ground and so reasons no guard is necessary. But it is more likely that being underground, he knows that though I may be able to hide, still I will not be able to escape. For that stone door which guards the entrance to this land in the roots of the mountain will certainly be both closed and guarded.'

He was uncertain what to do. If he left Vrilig and Skathrig to explore the corridors of the castle and consult with others of his company (if any could be found in possession of his senses), it would be easy for the Firbolg to take the weapons of his two sleeping companions. If on the other hand he stayed to guard them, he might lose forever an opportunity of attempting to find a way of escape for himself and his men and of contacting the others.

Despite the fact that they were lying in their armour on a floor of cold stone, his two roommates were sleeping deeply, flat on their backs, facing the light overhead in its globe of radiance. Noting this, Eusebius took their cloaks and put them over their faces and watched the effect. In a while Vrilig stirred, grunted, groped with a weak hand, pulled aside the cloak, and again settled back into slumber.

Eusebius now turned his attention to that pink warm sun, wondering whether this was the source of that power which had produced such a change in his men. Certainly as soon as they had entered the light of these pleasant groves, all his men had started to act strangely. When he gazed fully at it, he felt his mind melt like butter over a hot fire. Thought went, and with thought, all resolution and will. He retained only sufficient to withdraw his gaze, and shutting his eyes, shielded them further from the light with his hands. Then again his mind cleared and his thoughts arose out of the formless but pleasant feelings which had flooded his senses.

Having noted this, Eusebius now knew what to do. He took the cloaks of both Vrilig and Skathrig and blindfolded them so that none of that mind-lulling light could reach their eyes – even through their closed eyelids. Soon they stirred, groaned, wakened and then, in great distress, began retching, bringing up quantities of that black mushroom wine which they had drunk.

'Leave your eyes covered,' said Eusebius sternly. 'Keep them firmly shut. Believe me, your lives and those of your comrades depend on it.' In a little while both had to some extent recovered and Eusebius explained the situation to them.

'I am not myself affected by this light,' he said. 'But you plainly are. And here is a terrible plight indeed. Seeing, you are captives of the light; blind, you cannot find your way to freedom. Alas that so terrible a fate should have overtaken us.'

'Give me my sword and lead me blind among those little men,' stormed Vrilig. 'Even blinded I will make them fear the Geats forevermore.'

'What is not known immediately can certainly be found out by trial,' said Eusebius, ignoring this boast of the Geat. 'It is strange indeed that I am less affected by this light than you, for we are both men, though of different races. Also it seemed to me that you, Vrilig, were less affected than the others, and the Firbolg are least under the influence of those mind-bending rays, though I fancy they also are a little altered here below. Yet how can all this be?'

He studied the problem in silence but without getting an answer. 'What is the difference between a man from Phoenicia and one of the Vikings?' he demanded aloud, impatient that he could not find the answer.

'More to the point,' said Skathrig peevishly, 'what is the resemblance between a man from Phoenicia and one of the Firbolg?'

'That is simple,' said the Geat. 'Both have dark skins and both have hair black as the mane of a horse. If all riddles are as simple as that, I can be called a wizard.'

'That is it!' cried Eusebius. 'The hair. All Vikings are fair-haired. Thick dark hair prevents these rays entering the brain except through the eyes. And not enough enters by those doors alone to deprive the Firbolg or myself of our senses.'

'Well,' said Skathrig, still peevish perhaps from the amount of mushroom wine he had drunk, 'then if we can stay here long enough to grow black hair, we can take off our blindfolds and fight our way out.'

But the Geat, whose mind was most like that of the Phoenician, had already ripped off his blindfold and put his cloak over his head like a hood, his eyes shielded by it from the direct rays of the light. Eusebius watched him keenly. Vrilig reached for his sword and made it sing through the air. Then he turned on Skathrig, who had also removed his blindfold and shrouded his face in the folds of his cloak.

'Your singing, Skathrig, is the most villainous to which I have ever listened,' he snapped. 'The croaking of crows is pure melody compared with the sound of your cracked voice.'

Skathrig unlimbered his big double-bladed axe, and glaring at the redheaded sword-wielder growled, 'One more surly word and I will lop off your head and give you the gift of eternal silence.'

'It seems to me,' said Eusebius with a thin smile, 'that I have back at least two of my warriors in their proper senses. Come! Let us save the rest!'

Chapter 21

The Firbolg, it seemed, entirely trusted the mind-robbing light and the effect of the mushroom wine to guard their prisoners, for they had set no one to watch over them. The three then, two with their heads covered with their cloaks and their eyes shaded from that evil light, left the room carved of rock to which they had been assigned, and walking down the corridor outside searched in every room for their companions. They could not find them. Not a single door was bolted and not a single room was guarded, but all were empty.

The corridor made the complete circuit of the castle and they found not a trace of their companions nor a sign of any of the Firbolg. Back to the banqueting room they went, in the centre of the castle, but not a person was to be found. They listened, tense and expectant, but heard not a sound. The soft pinkish light flooded the entire banqueting hall. The tables were empty. The armour and weapons of men hanging on the walls of the adjacent hall gave terrible evidence of the fate that awaited them.

'I saw a staircase in the corridor,' said Eusebius. 'Let us go down that. If our comrades are anywhere in this accursed castle, they must certainly be in the dungeons.' The staircase, they discovered, lay in comparative darkness. It was a circular staircase, like a big tunnel connecting floor to floor, and it got its light only through the doors from the staircase to each floor.

The stairs were worn and small, built for the Firbolg.

The three went down them with great difficulty. As they descended the light diminished and the air grew cold and damp. They passed three levels, each with an opening from the stairs to a floodlit but empty room. Past the third level they went, down into the darkness and chill.

'Beware lest they have some dragon down below,' said Skathrig. 'Dragons are known to live in just such a place as this – in the bowels of mountains. Also they do the bidding of dwarfs such as these Firbolg.'

'No dragon ever got down this staircase,' said Eusebius. 'Keep your weapons ready. And remember, do not look directly at the light nor let its rays reach your heads.'

After a little while, still going down with great care, the light increased. But it was no longer that baleful light of the upper castle, but the flickering ruddy light of torches that now greeted them. They came, at the foot of the stairs, to a dripping dungeon, low-ceilinged and foul-smelling. In the walls of this place were torches in cressets. And chained to the walls, by hands and feet, were their companions, some groaning, some in a deep stupor. All were weaponless and many missing their armour.

'These men are twice fettered,' said Eusebius. 'They were fettered once with chains and again with the stupor into which they have sunk from that light and the mushroom wine.' He plucked a torch from the wall and passed along the men, seeing if any of them were sufficiently conscious to be of any aid. But though they stirred and groaned, none could be brought to their senses. Eusebius then examined the locks by which they were chained by their hands and their feet and the Geat also gave these his attention. But Skathrig saw that all were fastened to a bar of metal which ran along the wall and was itself locked in a socket. If this could be undone they would be able to move about though still with chains on hands or feet.

'We must find their jailer and the key,' said Vrilig.

'I have as good a key as ever you will find,' said Skathrig, and swung his mighty war axe at the master lock. In two powerful blows that filled the whole dungeon with the ringing of the axe, he had broken the lock. Quickly he threw aside the central bar and all were free of it, though still individually fettered.

While Skathrig had been busy with this good work, Eusebius had crept to the door by which the staircase entered the dungeon. As he expected, two of the Firbolg came running down the staircase. One he knocked to the ground with the hilt of his sword (for, like a woman, he did not like to kill) and the other he seized by the neck and soon had prisoner.

'Search that one for the keys,' he told Vrilig, who indeed found a large key on the man who had been knocked to the ground. But it was useless, being the key to that lock which Skathrig had already burst open with his axe.

'Where is the other key?' Eusebius demanded from the Firbolg he had captured. But the dwarf would not reply.

'Bring the torch here,' said Eusebius, 'and hold this fellow. He will soon find that two can play games with light.'

Skathrig held the dwarf and Eusebius took the torch.

'Now,' said the Phoenician, 'tell me where the key is, or I will so light your face with this torch that you will lose your senses quicker than my Norsemen.'

'Gro Me'ak has it!' cried their prisoner. 'Do not harm me. It is in his chamber. I will take you there.' The other, knocked to the ground, had now recovered and swore that what his companion said was true. Gro Me'ak trusted none with keys, but kept them in his own chamber, which was on the top floor of the castle.

'Yet you had one key,' said Eusebius suspiciously.

'Only the key to release them from the dungeon so they could be taken to their work,' said the Firbolg. 'The key to release their hands and legs Gro Me'ak keeps himself.'

'Let us go and find Gro Me'ak,' said Vrilig. 'Indeed I was right in my first thought about him. He's so small a man I should have doubled him by splitting him in half with my sword, as I wished to do when he brought his ant men against us.'

'First we will look further here,' said Eusebius. 'Perhaps we will find something of use.'

They first tied up the two jailers and then searched the dungeon with their torch. Their fettered companions now began to recover their senses and pleaded to be released. They first thought Eusebius and the others were Firbolgs, for the flickering torch gave but an uncertain light. But when they discovered their true identity, they shouted their names with joy and struggled against their bonds. Skathrig indeed set about freeing them individually by striking their chains apart with his great axe. He needed a steady hand and better light to be sure that he did not cut off an arm or a leg in this good work, for the chains, though strong, were short.

Still some of the Norsemen agreed cheerfully that the loss of an arm or a leg would be a small price to pay for freedom. 'Strike hard,' Knute encouraged Skathrig. 'Odin will without doubt guide your blow. One-handed and free I may still find a worthier death than rotting with both hands whole in this foul place.'

'I would sooner lose foot than hand,' said another Norseman. 'Eric the Lame has done well with but one good foot to stand on.'

'And where is he?' asked Eusebius. 'I do not see him among you.'

'That we do not know,' they replied. 'He was taken away, being less enchanted than the rest of us.'

'When you leave here,' warned Eusebius, 'be sure to keep your head and eyes covered from the lights of the Firbolg. And drink no more of that foul mushroom wine.'

He went off then, leaving Skathrig to work at the freeing of the others with his mighty axe. A tunnel led from the dungeon through the thick walls, and listening at its entrance, he fancied he could hear faint cries coming to him.

The tunnel was so small that he could not enter it standing and Vrilig besought him not to enter it at all. 'Be sure that at the other end you will find some monster of the Firbolg – perhaps that dragon of which the son of the priestess of Odin has already warned you.' He made mention of Skathrig in this way to remind the Phoenician that that one had special powers of foreseeing the future.

'You may remain if you wish,' said Eusebius. 'But I have never seen a dragon. Truly I would repent all the days of my life if I returned to my own country having come so far to hear of such a monster and then turned back through fear.'

'It is surprising that I should teach one like you the difference between fear and wisdom,' said Vrilig. 'Who stirs the sleeping dragon is not a brave man but a fool.'

'That is true,' said Eusebius. 'I will take the torch and go quietly.' Stooping down, he entered the tunnel and the Geat came in after him, for he would not let it be said that he had let the Stranger go where he dared not follow.

The tunnel went upwards for some distance, making it difficult to go along, for the floor was wet and slippery. Then it turned first to the right, then to the left, and then to the right again. Then it descended and the Phoenician, thinking on these turns, decided that the tunnel had been built after the castle was erected and went in these directions to avoid going through pillars, which would weaken these supports.

A scent not altogether unfamiliar now reached their nostrils in that wet and cold air. It was the smell of that black mushroom wine of which their companions had drunk so deeply. They soon heard the cries which had attracted their attention coming louder and louder, though still muffled by the closeness of the tunnel. The flickering torch, turning at times blue in the heavy air, threw little light and gave them no view of what lay ahead. But at last the tunnel widened so that they were able to stand and soon, going down three small steps, they found themselves in a place heavy with fumes of the mushroom wine but so large that the light of the torch did not reach either the walls about or the ceiling.

The piteous cries, however, were now very loud and close, but coming from ahead of them. Slowly they walked towards these and found a surprising sight. Chained to a wall of this dungeon, as had been their own companions, were scores of Firbolgs, many of them old men and women, some of them only boys and girls.

At the sight of the intruders, these all stopped their clamour and gazed in amazement at Eusebius and Vrilig.

'Are you friends to Lancelot – did Arthur send you?' asked one old dwarf whose ravaged face seemed all the older in the torchlight.

'Lancelot we know only by name,' said Eusebius. 'Arthur we know, but he did not send us. Who are you?'

'I am Ku Melin, one-time King of the Firbolg, and these are all who are loyal to me and who resisted that traitor Gro Me'ak when he seized power with the aid of my army, which he turned against me. If you are friend to Gro Me'ak, we are lost. But if you are, as you say, a friend to Arthur, then free us, I beg of you.'

'That I would gladly do if I had but the key to your chains,' said Eusebius.

'It is over against that wall,' said Ku Melin. 'There are two. One which unlocks us from these bars and another which unlocks our fetters and manacles.' The keys were soon found and the prisoners set free.

'If any of your comrades were overcome by the mushroom wine and the light and were chained as we were, these same keys will free them,' said Ku Melin.

'Let us quickly get back to Skathrig,' said Vrilig. 'If we can release our comrades and get to that great chamber where are kept the arms of others less fortunate than ourselves, we may be able to win our way out of this underground world. What would I not give at this moment for a sight of the sun and the smell of the sea?'

'Does the sun indeed still shine on the surface?' asked Ku Melin. 'I had forgotten that so great a blessing existed.'

'It shines,' said Eusebius. 'But between us and the sight of it lies a mountain of stone. Therefore let us make haste.'

Chapter 22

All the Norsemen were soon freed with the same key that had loosed the captive Firbolg and their king. It was not true that Gro Me'ak alone had the keys that would lose their fetters. The jailers had lied on this score and to pay them back (and also prevent them spreading the alarm) they were themselves chained in the fetters which had been used on the Norsemen.

Eusebius, ever cautious, now debated what next to do. 'It would be foolish to try to leave this dungeon as we entered by that winding staircase,' he said. 'The shaft is so small that but one of us can go at a time. It would be an easy matter to capture each man as he emerged, and that also being true of anyone coming down the staircase is no doubt the reason why none have come down after those two jailers. We are awaited by that narrow door where the stair enters the Great Hall. Also, we are unarmed except for three among us. Better for us to think and debate now than to act and lose that measure of freedom which we have won.'

'As for being unarmed,' said Skathrig, 'each man can take with him those chains which once bound him. They will be weapon enough until we get better.'

'Is there no other way out of these dungeons?' asked Eusebius of Ku Melin.

'None,' said the old king. 'For that reason no guard need stay in the dungeons, since it is necessary only to guard the exit from the staircase. However, there is an exit from the staircase on each floor of the castle and there are five floors. If we could contrive to get up the stairs to each of those exits, then there would be five for Gro Me'ak and his men to guard.'

'Small task for so large a force,' said Eusebius. 'He could hold each exit with half a dozen men. Tell me, of what are the Firbolg mostly afraid?'

'Darkness,' said Ku Melin. 'It is for that reason that all is lighted in our underground world.'

'And their principal weapon?' asked Eusebius.

'The sling,' replied Ku Melin. 'With that they are skilful beyond belief. Or perhaps you have seen already how with a sling the cliff face that guards the entrance to the world of the Firbolg is lowered.'

'That we have seen indeed and marvelled at,' said Eusebius. 'Now it seems to me that I see a way to freedom and safety, and you, Vrilig, will certainly soon regret that you ever scorned that special weapon which I carry and which can, like the slings of the Firbolg, strike from a distance. Let us go up these stairs now, but I will go ahead. It is fortunate indeed that I was able to keep bow and arrows from our treacherous hosts.'

They mounted the stairs then quickly, the Phoenician ahead with an arrow to his bowstring. None could shield him from the expected stones of the Firbolg slingers, who would without doubt loose these missiles at him as soon he appeared in the doorway of the staircase. Only his own skill and swiftness could save him. Certainly the Firbolg would know of his coming however quietly he moved up the stairs.

Now did the Stranger in his coloured cloak show his wiliness to the Vikings once more. For approaching that last bend of the staircase before the door, he stepped quickly around it into the light that came from a hall and immediately withdrew. Instantly there was a hail of stones from the Firbolg slingers which rattled off the curved walls of the staircase, darting from side to side but injuring none, for their first force was soon spent.

As soon as this storm had passed the Phoenician stepped again into the light, and stretching his bow, sped an arrow at the light of that hall. Aimed surely, the dart whistled through the air and struck a glowing globe, shattering it to pieces. Another dart followed the first, shattering a second globe, and the hall was reduced to a gloom like that of a stormy sunset.

There was no need now for the Phoenician to withdraw from the stones of the slingers. Amazed, their aim rendered uncertain by the gloom, they scattered, and out of that hole of a door from the staircase came the Vikings so like hunting wolves, brandishing those chains which had ignobly fettered them. The light no longer menaced them, being so greatly reduced, and they soon found that by itself the light had only a small effect on their natures. The dark wine of the mushrooms was the real worker of evil.

Soon the Vikings had control both of the banqueting hall and of the Great Hall adjoining it, and had armed themselves with better weapons than chains. Swords and spears they found in abundance, also good helmets plumed with horsehair and corselets of metal plates riveted to leather, after the style of the Romans. The Jutes were especially heartened to have again spears in their hands and made great slaughter with them, singing their spear song, which is all riddles and which goes in part as follows:

> Guarding it stands but fighting lies down
> Here is a tree that flies around
> Grows not an inch. Its fruit is red.
> It reaps its harvest by rooting its head.

Such grim jokes about their weapon gave added delight to the Jutes in their fighting, for they were unlike the Swedes and Geats, who preferred not to waste the splendid time of combat with childish games but called always on the gods to witness the greatness of their blows.

From the Great Hall a broad staircase led to the upper floors and the Vikings stormed this over the bodies of their foes, only to be met by a shattering storm of stones from the slings of the Firbolg who had recovered their courage on the upper floors. Many of the Vikings were struck to the ground by these missiles and fell back upon their comrades on the staircase. Then, through the door leading from the courtyard to the Great Hall, came more of the Firbolg, led by that other leader of theirs, Drogith by name, who had, with a stone from his sling moved the cliff that led to the underground world of these small creatures. He and his followers rode in on their small horses, brandishing hammer, spear, and axe, and so mounted, were a good match for the Vikings, now trapped on the staircase from above and below.

'Praise and glory to all the gods,' cried Vrilig, seeing them so beset. 'Give room now for the sword of a Geat. Odin, I charge you, put down your horn of mead and watch a Geat while he cuts his path towards you.' So he swung his mighty sword like the flail of a thresher around his head and the Firbolg fell back or fell under his assault.

Nor did the others hold back, but flung themselves on their foes, exulting both in the ferocity of the fighting and the odds by which they were outnumbered. 'None can be ashamed to speak of this now,' cried Skathrig. 'It is reasonable to count three of these manikins as one – one, two, three.' So he counted those who fell to his iron axe of war and bade Thor, who himself favoured this weapon, to watch closely how he did his business.

Hjalmar, one of the Danes, also did fine work with a sword of the Romans, though he mourned the shortness of the blade, which could be used only for stabbing. And in all that clamour Eusebius worked quietly with that small sword, Wasp, surrounded by enemies and bleeding from wounds he had received from their swords.

The stand which the Vikings had taken upon the great staircase favoured them in dealing with their enemies from below, those led by Drogith, but put them at a disadvantage in dealing with others who had come down the staircase from the upper places of the castle. Here having to fight, as it were, above their heads, and handicapped in trying to advance over the bodies of those of their foes (and some also of their own) who had fallen at their feet, they were at last beaten back step by step upon those below them.

Now indeed it seemed that they would be killed to the last man, for more and more of the Firbolg crowded about them, and those loyal to Ku Melin who had been released from the dungeon were themselves cut off from the Vikings and were fighting for their lives with what weapons they could seize.

Then above the shouting and the ring and clash of weapons came three strident blasts upon a war horn. So brazen and loud were these blasts that they struck fear into the hearts of the Firbolg while greatly heartening the embattled Vikings. And then at the head of the stair appeared Eric the Lame, holding in one hand the head of that treacherous usurper and enslaver of his guests, Gro Me'ak.

Dismay spread instantly through the horde of the Firbolg. Nor were they given a chance to recover from their surprise. The Vikings turned on them once more, more savage than wolves, and those leaderless dwarfs threw away their weapons and fled. Soon all had left but Drogith and a few of his companions and these, seeing their cause hopeless, put down their weapons and surrendered.

But Drogith would not give his sword to Eusebius or any of his companions, but only to Eric the Lame. And in so doing, he made this apology, 'I was misled by my loyalty to a prophecy among our people which said that they would be freed from tyranny for all time by half a man. I therefore followed Gro Me'ak when he bade us rise against Ku Melin who, whatever he has told you, was not without fault when he ruled over us. But I see now that the half a man foretold in that prophecy was none other than this lame one. To him then I surrender and to him alone I pledge my loyalty, I will serve no other.'

These words were met by shouts of approval by others of the Firbolg who remained in the Great Hall, and they greeted Eric the Lame, not Eusebius, as their true conqueror.

Chapter 23

So it was that Eric the Lame, who in his homeland had been thought fit only to act the part of ploughman, bound to the dull earth and the slow oxen, had gained for himself a kingdom among the Firbolg – if he wanted it. For all of these people were of the same opinion as Drogith, their captain; namely, that they would trust none to reign over them in the future but this Norseman, who being lame from birth was considered but half a man among his own people.

Drogith showed to the Norsemen the stone on which the prophecy concerning their king was carved. The Vikings could not, of course, read the script of the stone, for they were familiar only with runic script. The script of the Firbolg was called Ogham and consisted of a line with a number of cuts made either above or below it – the position and number of these cuts indicating the sound of the word so written. This stone was placed over the great entrance to the castle and according to Drogith (his word was hardly to be doubted since he translated in the midst of his fellows) it read as follows:

> Men of the Firbolg, await the day
> When half meets half, takes half away
> And remaining half is also whole
> Then will terror cease its toll.

The Vikings thought this a poor prophecy, for the words were not cunning and the prophecy could as easily refer to one of the Firbolg as to Eric the Lame. But the Firbolg (against whose dark natures Arthur had cautioned Eusebius) were by no means ready to accept rule again by one of their own people. Too much drinking of their strange wine had rotted their characters and they were sure that only someone from the surface would rule wisely and justly over them. It seemed that Ku Melin had been as much of a tyrant in his day as Gro Me'ak, who had overthrown him. If Drogith now succeeded Gro Me'ak, he would, all were sure, turn tyrant himself in a while.

'Are you prepared to trust yourself among so doubtful a people?' asked Eusebius in talking of this to Eric. 'Think well. The price of a kingdom is too often the death of the king.'

'Alone I will certainly not put on their crown,' said Eric. 'But if I might have five or six of my own to join me as a bodyguard, then certainly this is a fine booty of war for a ploughman. It is entirely unlikely that I will ever again be offered a kingdom – even underground.'

'We have lost four or five good men,' said Eusebius. 'Yet perhaps four or five others might pledge themselves to you, if not for life, then for a certain time until others are attracted to your following. Be sure that I will not speak against it if some of those with me should desire to take up that service.'

Word then was passed among the Norsemen that those who wished to enter the service of Eric the Lame, King of the Firbolg, might do so. Two of the Jutes immediately stated they were prepared to follow Eric and also a Dane, a Swede, and a Finn. But none of the Vikings, that is to say, the Geats or those who lived more by sea than by land, would accept such service. Already they longed for the sea and the roar of the waves, the boom and shout of the rude wind, and the hiss of their longships through the tumbling ocean water.

But before the company parted (Eric having firmly decided to remain as King of the Firbolg), those who had died in the battle on the staircase had to be given a proper funeral.

The men's bodies were carried on litters out of that land of pearly light into the bright and active sunlight above. The quick clean wind caressed them and blew their long golden hair over their faces, now turned to grey stone. There were seven of these dead, all now with Odin, and knowing that though dead they were watching from Valhalla, their companions, not to disgrace them before the gods, gave them an excellent funeral.

They built a pyre which was six feet high and twelve feet square, constructed of great logs with much underbrush laid about. On top of this pyre they laid the pleasant boughs of trees and the leaves of ferns to make a good bed for these warriors in death.

Then they laid out each man beside his shield, his sword, and his helmet, and clad in his corselet of ring mail. Those of the Firbolg who had fallen to their weapons they laid around them, to be their servants in Valhalla. Then Skathrig lighted a torch to set the pyre ablaze but waited until Eusebius had pronounced the praises of each man who had died. Their comrades then added to the pyre such weapons as they could spare for their friends. Now Skathrig, with a shout to attract the attention of the gods, put the torch to the pyre.

Soon the all-consuming flames reached with their bright tongues towards these noble dead. First a pillar of smoke rose from the fire hiding the bodies completely and reaching upwards to the clouds. Then the base of this pillar disappeared in flames, yellow and red, which rising higher and higher produced such a heat that none could stand close by. So to the roaring of the flames and the sounding of war horns were the dead of the Battle of the Firbolg given their funeral. After these solemn ceremonies, Eric was crowned King of the Firbolg and a great coronation feast was given the same evening.

At this feast, however, Eric gave strictest instructions that none of that evil wine of mushrooms was to be given to the Vikings, and he made it a law in his kingdom that this malevolent brew should never be given to himself or to any of his followers. Also it was to be drunk by the Firbolg themselves only sparingly and most of the extensive fields of mushrooms previously planted were torn up and resowed with innocent and healthy crops.

At this feast Drogith and Ku Melin undertook to explain to Eusebius many of the mysteries of their people. Regarding the mushroom wine, they said that its use was recent, it having been produced for the first time only a thousand years previously – a short time in the history of the Firbolg. Before that time, the Firbolg regarded all mushrooms as poisonous and suitable only as the pale food of the spirits of the dead who still roamed the earth. In those days they cultivated few crops but kept herds of goats, sheep, swine, and cattle. However, with the coming of invaders who drove them underground, they found that the mushrooms were at first the only crops they could raise. In great hunger they had been driven at last to eating them and found through use that some produced a feeling of well-being while others produced a feeling of rage.

'We learned to avoid those that produced only rage and eat those that gave us a feeling of safety and friendliness,' said Drogith. 'But we found also that these same mushrooms robbed us of our will, and after eating them we were for several days without energy or purpose. Therefore it was decreed that they should be used only in the form of wine and served only at great banquets when no event of any importance had to be put in hand immediately after. From this it was but a short step to using the mushroom wine to enslave others. Many have been the slaves of this brew and those so enslaved, either on purpose or through their own surrender to the wine, were put to work tilling our fields. For under the spell of the mushroom wine, they feel no pain and no fatigue, though worked hard in this way they do not live long.

'We of the Firbolg, however, have now built up some resistance to the effects of this wine. Therefore our new king would be wise not to be too harsh in administering the rules against drinking it.'

'I make no rule against the drinking of the mushroom wine by the men of the Firbolg,' said Eric the Lame. 'But I make this rule concerning its effects – that if any man, as a result of drinking the mushroom wine, cannot perform his proper work or do the service required of him by his community, then he will be punished by one day's imprisonment for every hour of incapacity. Therefore drink all you wish. I rule not against drinking but against the effects of drinking.'

At these words many of the Firbolg pushed their goblets of wine from them. Eusebius, leaning across to Eric, said, 'You speak wisely. No man can, under such a rule, feel himself forced one way or another. Each is the judge of his own ability in the matter of drinking the wine. Out of that a true control may well come.' He then turned to Ku Melin to question him about the source of that strange light with which the whole underground world of the Firbolg was lit.

'Those globes, as you see,' said Ku Melin, 'produce not

only light but health for man, for beast, and for all growing things. You have perhaps noted that the light soothes the mind and makes a man friendly to his neighbour. This property of light we discovered many centuries ago when it was the custom to light particular places with lights of different colours to lend variety. It was found that when we stayed long in a chamber lit with red light, we became irritated and suspicious. Many quarrels broke out in that chamber and many were killed in it as a result. Also we found that blue light made us sad and uncommunicative. But the light we now use, we found, produced good feeling and trust and so that colour was decided upon and is now used completely.

'Now as to the source of the light. It comes from a particular kind of air – of which there are many seepages from the centre of the earth – to be found in this underground land. This air, when it is heated slightly, glows with the light that you see, but is never consumed. The globes are made of crystal by our craftsmen, who alone know how to fill the globes with this glowing air and then seal them. These lights never dim, and those in this banquet hall (other than the new ones replacing those broken by your weapon) are said to be seven hundred years old.'

'How are these globes heated?' asked Eusebius. 'I see no fire near them.'

'They get sufficient heat from the warmth of this hall, which is itself warmed by the fire and by our bodies,' said Ku Melin. 'Now you can understand why these lights never go out. The temperature of our underground world would have to drop greatly before the lights ceased glowing. Indeed, we first found this air in a small cave, utterly dark, in which a pale glow appeared when we had been in it a little time and the cave had been warmed by the fire we lit.'

This explanation greatly interested the Phoenician, but the Norsemen laughed and said that they had many times at sea in their longships seen balls of light settle on their masts and pass up and down and even along the shield wall around the sides of the ship and then disappear.

'They are Thor's lanterns,' they said. 'These little men have only found a way to capture them.'

The Phoenician also, in voyages in his merchant ships carrying cargoes of scented wood, ape skins, ivory, and vials of the purple blood of mussels used in dyeing cloth, had seen such balls of fire about the masts and even rolling over the deck in particular conditions of weather, but most often before storms. But they were thought, among his people, to be the life-essence of those who had drowned in the sea. However, he did not dispute the matter with his comrades, finding that the Norsemen particularly resented any suggestion that their own beliefs might be in error.

Ku Melin now inquired what was the purpose of Eusebius and his band in coming to their land, and what was his relationship with Arthur, and whether he was not, like Lancelot before him, in the service of that king. Because he knew the nature of the Firbolg to be unreliable, and perhaps as a result of living underground, tending to treachery or at least malice, Eusebius was not at first willing to answer these questions frankly. He explained how he had pledged to restore the authority of Arthur and had done so in the eastern and southern portions of the White Island.

'But surely you have not undertaken so dangerous and arduous a task out of good nature,' said Ku Melin slyly. 'Some reward must certainly be promised for so great a service.'

'He has agreed to give us certain lands on which my people can settle,' said Eusebius.

'Indeed?' said Ku Melin. 'And yet it seems to me that so formidable a group as you, if you are able to subdue the king's lands for him, might subdue them for yourselves, and take over the kingdom of Arthur rather than restore it to him. Surely then, there is some other payment involved.'

'As you see,' said Eusebius, 'he has rewarded my men with a great quantity of weapons and war gear of many kinds. And he has also given them rings and bracelets and armbands and amulets and other things in which they delight.'

'And perhaps – the promise of a certain Cup for yourself?' said Ku Melin, watching Eusebius out of the corner of his eye.

The mention of this Cup, by all means the sole object of the Phoenician's expedition, startled Eusebius, and dropping now all pretences, he looked directly at the aged face of Ku Melin, former King of the Firbolg and said, 'What do you know about this Cup, for you are right in guessing that it is that which I seek.'

'Did not Arthur tell you that it was that same Cup which first scattered his Round Table and his company of knights?' asked Ku Melin.

'No,' said Eusebius. 'He promised he would help me find it. That promise he did not keep, but remained behind at Camelot. Indeed he spoke little of this Cup and then only obscurely, as a man who knows much but doubts how his knowledge will be received.'

'Be assured that those who seek this Cup never return from their quest the same men. Whether they find it or not, they are changed – some greatly, some only subtly. And yet who is to say that any change is subtle or small? For what is changed, even in the slightest degree, is never again what it once was. And it is the nature of change, that once made, it cannot be erased.'

'In what way are they changed?' demanded Eusebius.

'In this way,' said Ku Melin. 'All they have valued before becomes of no importance to them. So it was that those knights of the king who set out to seek this Cup called Grail never again returned to the king's service nor delighted in tournaments of deeds of arms. Some were indeed slain but others became monks or hermits or wanderers over the earth. Lancelot went mad, I am told. And what of the rest of them – even those who did not seek the Cup? Are they not all dead and nothing more now than a memory – all save Arthur? And Arthur is not now what he once was. He is only a shadow, so I hear, a tattered remembrance of that great king who once ruled so gloriously in this land.'

'You seem well informed in these matters,' said Eusebius.

'So I am indeed,' said Ku Melin. 'As you see I am now an old man, and I was alive when the Cup was first brought here seven hundred years ago. We of the Firbolg live a great time compared with your insignificant lives. Nor do we stay entirely below ground, but some of us, as spies, move about on the surface, observing and listening to what is happening among the most recent invaders of what is our island.

'That Cup was brought here by one Joseph of Arimathea when I was a boy. He took it to that place called Avalon in Lyonnesse in the western part of this island and there lived with it in a cell. He also put into the ground the stick with which he walked and that stick became a tree which flowers each midwinter night.'

'There are many such trees,' said the Phoenician suspiciously. 'There are in certain areas of the world trees which flower only every seventh year and others which flower but once and then, if they are to flower again, must be burned completely to the ground. What of this Cup which can give everlasting life to whoever can drink from it? Where is it to be found for certain? Does Arthur have it himself, as I sometimes suspect?'

'All we know of this Cup is that it is never found anywhere but at this place called Avalon,' said Ku Melin. 'Nor does Arthur have that Cup, as you suspect. No man has it. For the Cup appears and disappears, showing itself to some and not to others. Perhaps you will see it. Perhaps you will not. But of one thing you can be sure. You will never again be that same person who first set out to seek this vessel.'

'As to that,' said Eusebius, 'I am still myself and unchanged.'

'If that is true,' said Ku Melin, 'why have you come to this island? You should be with your merchant ships, carrying precious goods for sale across the ocean.'

'To that life I can return at will, and will certainly do so when I have this Cup, the Grail.'

'To that life,' said Ku Melin gravely, 'you can never return again.'

Chapter 24

'Eric the Lame, Ku Melin, and about five hundred of those dwarfs over whom Eric now ruled by their consent, accompanied Eusebius and his men the following day to the borders of the Singing Hills to set them on their way to Glastonbury.

'A day's riding will bring you to Avalon,' said Ku Melin. 'Half a day more and you will find Lyonnesse in the west. The Great Road of the West leads directly to Avalon. It lies, as you see from your map, on an island in the centre of a lake. The island is now called the Island of Avalon, which means, in the language of the Cymri (who once owned it) the Island of Apples or the Island of Happiness. But among us, who are the oldest people here, it has another name.'

'What name?' asked Eusebius.

'Isgish Dubga,' said Ku Melin. 'That is to say, the Island of the Dead.'

'And why does it have such a name?' asked Eusebius.

'It is said that on that island, Death first began his reign upon earth, and all living creatures, including ourselves, became mortal.'

Eusebius considered this gravely for some time and then said, 'It is fitting that the Cup of Life should be found on the Island of the Dead, for all things exist in the presence of their opposites. Now I begin to understand that riddle of Arthur concerning Life being the mother of Death and Death the mother also of Life. That old ruler is wiser than I had given him credit for. But what was meant by the wizard Merlin when he sent me the message that mortality of man is the greatest of wisdom escapes me yet.'

From this time, Eusebius became more grave. He talked less with his men, fell into deep thought, and rode for a long time in silence, some distance from the others. He laughed less and no longer encouraged them by witticisms and by taunts to press forward on the Great Road of the West. After parting with Ku Melin and Eric, he seemed in no haste but rather dallied. Thus by the end of that first day they had not yet come to the borders of Lyonnesse and they made camp on a hilltop by the side of the Great Road of the West, where the Norsemen had soon lit a big fire for their comfort, to ward off wild beasts and to cook their dinners. The horses were tethered and left under guard in a hollow nearby, and after supper Vrilig made mention of the solemn mood which had come over Eusebius.

'It seems to me that you may even now be undergoing that change which overcame the warriors of Arthur when they sought the Cup of Life,' he said. 'Perhaps, however, it is not too late. You should certainly be free to decide whether to go to this accursed Island of the Dead or turn back. It seems to me that no reasonable man will go to such a place when still in the prime of his life. My advice to you is to turn back from this quest and return to Lug's Dun where our fine ships are still waiting for us. A day or two on the life-giving ocean will soon give you a better view of the world.'

'It is not possible for any man to avoid his Weird and it is not seemly for him to try to do so,' countered Skathrig. 'Even if a man were to succeed in avoiding whatever death or misfortune is in store for him, how can he live

179

afterward, having run away like a coward? Who will listen to his boast or stand shoulder to shoulder with him in the thickest part of the battle? Such a man is in truth already dead, and worse than that, is dead without honour.'

Eusebius, the firelight flickering on his hawk-face, made no comment on these speculations.

'For myself,' said Vrilig, 'I believe a man should live as long as he can. If he can avoid death without cowardice, but by guile or strategem, then he is entitled to do so. However, if death is unavoidable except by cowardice, then a man should die. I certainly have no fear of death, though there are some who have such a fear.' He glanced at Eusebius as he said these words.

'Neither have I any fear except to die in my bed or of some miserable illness which would rob me of my strength and yet leave me alive,' said Skathrig. 'To die in such a way is certainly the greatest misfortune. Better by far to be drowned or crushed by a falling rock or tree.'

'I believe that I am now approaching my own death,' said Eusebius. 'If this is true, let Vrilig take command of the men and let him go back to Lug's Dun so that Knute and all those who wish to return to their homeland may do so on *Black Gull* and *Cormorant*. Let him also pass by the Singing Hills and speak with Eric the Lame and those who remained with him, lest he also wishes to return to his homeland. For reigning as King of the Firbolg may not always suit his pleasure.'

'Although you are not a Viking, I will be sorry if you die,' said Vrilig quietly. 'Also, since you are not a Viking, it is perhaps not so strange that you should be afraid of dying and so have become silent at death's approach. I would not be afraid myself, since I have performed enough feats of arms to be taken immediately to Valhalla, but I can understand why you should be afraid, for you do not know of such a place, and what Valkyrie will take you there?'

'I am not afraid,' said Eusebius quietly. 'I am concerned only with the meaning of death. I am troubled not that I should die, if indeed that is what is in store for me, but rather about understanding why I should die. For so great a thing as death must certainly have a meaning equally great. It cannot be senseless.'

'You started this quest seeking not death but life,' said Skathrig. 'You set out to find the Cup of Life. Do you now despair of finding that Cup? Or do you think that you have been deeply deceived concerning it?'

'I have been pondering the significance of that Cup and remembering what Arthur said concerning life – that it is the parent of death. And also that death then is the parent of life. And now I see that one may not be had without the other. Therefore to drink from this Cup of Life is to ensure my death. He who first drank from it died himself and by torture, which is a mystery to me. Only then did he return to life. It seems then that I must die and perhaps in that same way in order to be restored to life and not die again. It is on that that I ponder. As for death itself, how can any man fear that which is common to every man?'

'You should turn back,' said Vrilig. 'It is foolishness to go on.'

'So near to the solution of so great a mystery, no man could turn back,' said Eusebius gravely. 'I tell you that if you put me now back in my own land, I would start out again on this same search. For this search would lure every man all the days of his life, if he but thought about it. Of what use is life if we do not know the meaning of life? I believe that on the Island of Avalon I will at last find the meaning.'

Vrilig looked at him quietly and then, changing the

subject, said, 'Tomorrow I trust that we kill a deer. I grow tired of dried meat.'

They passed a peaceful night and on the following day, after journeying for five hours, came upon the country of Lyonnesse. The Great Road of the West plunged straight into this country of water, rushes, marsh marigolds, wild flax, and yellow iris. Ahead and all about nothing could be seen but this watery countryside, in paths of dark green, light yellow, pale blue, and silver – a countryside then both lovely and sad, populated by waterfowl in vast numbers. Wild duck whistled by in their arrow formations and great white swans sailed across the blue sky to glide gracefully onto the surface of the deeper meres. Moorhens splashed and clucked on their little mud islands, glistening with sunlit water as they searched for their food. Ragged pennons of geese trailed across the sky, which was mirrored in the serene surface of the lakes. There was such a kinship between water and sky, flowers and clouds, waterfowl and the reflections of waterfowl, whether flying above the lakes or resting on their surface, that it seemed that with but a little change one would be turned into the other, or the two – waterland and sky – would become one.

In such a place only the Norsemen with their boars' head helmets and corselets of rusting ring mail looked unreal. The clumping of their horses' hoofs on the surface of the road and the clink of armour and of harness were sounds utterly foreign to that whole place.

'Truly in this pleasant land we alone are strangers,' said Eusebius with a smile. 'And yet for myself I feel that I am nearing home.'

'As for me,' said Skathrig, 'I would like to see one good strong tree in all this pretty woman's puddle. Or a rock that would make a sword blade ring when struck. Is that ten bridges we have passed since dawn?'

'Thirteen,' said Eusebius. 'But I see yonder the end of our journey.' He halted, rose in his stirrups, and pointed ahead. By doing likewise his companions could see a small purple island set in the middle of a silver lake.

'There lies Avalon,' he said. 'The Island of Happiness or the Island of the Dead. Perhaps indeed the two are after all not opposites but the same, differently viewed. Birth and death, then, may be but the same door, differently entered.'

Chapter 25

A small boat floated like a curled dried leaf at the border
of the lake in which the Island of Avalon was situated. The
waters of the lake were utterly still except for wavelets so
small that they scarcely moved the grains of sand as they
expended their elfin energy on the shore. The island was
little more than the peak of a rounded hill, the base sub-
merged in the crystal water, the peak mirrored to perfec-
tion in the lake.

From the top of this islet grew three tall fir trees, devoid
of branches except at their heads. The slim trunks, utterly
straight, were reproduced in the surface of the lake in
three slim lines. All things about the lake were doubled in
this manner. The little boat at the shore floated on its own
image, the rushes and flags on the margin or in the shallow
water grew out of their doubles, and in the depth of the
lake was the same sky which lay overhead – infinite and un-
reachable and clothed in clouds of purple, of gold and silver.

This world reflecting a world profoundly affected the
Phoenician, and turning to Skathrig he asked, 'Tell me,
son of a priestess of Odin, of that which lies before you
– which is real and which a reflection?' But Skathrig, watching a white heron which stood on one leg in the water,
itself examining its own perfect reflection, said, 'Both are
bound one to the other. They may not be separated.'

'You have spoken the first clear truth of our journey,'
said Eusebius. 'I will go now to this island and see if there
I find that which I seek.'

'Let me come with you, for you may need help, and it is unworthy that you should go into danger without a single companion,' said Vrilig.

'Into birth and into death each man journeys alone,' said Eusebius. 'Therefore you cannot come with me. Nor I with you when you make that journey.' He then entered the boat, and taking up the oars, pushed himself into the deeps of the lake and rowed on its silvered surface towards the island which lay, it seemed, but a short distance away.

From the bow and stern of the boat dark ripples now spread across the water, small indeed, and yet in that infinite calm of the lake, strongly marked. Each dip of the oars made its perfect ring in the silver water and each ring spread outwards, the widening circumference of each cutting across that of its neighbour to produce a graceful moving pattern of rings and lines upon the lake.

Eusebius found that the boat went readily, and the mood of sadness which had settled upon him the previous day was replaced by one of peace. He beached the boat in a little bay of white sand on the Island of Avalon, and unbuckling his sword, left it in the leaflike boat together with his shield. He turned for one last look of farewell at his comrades, who stood solid and black in the distance on the shore of the lake, and then he plunged through a screen of verdant ferns and golden willows towards the interior of the island. No bird fluttered away, disturbed by his coming; no frightened rabbit scuttled through the brush. The profound silence of the enchanted place seemed to completely absorb the sounds he made himself, and he felt that he was approaching a dimension which lay on the other side of silence and in which perhaps communication could be made without either sound or movement.

A little trail led from the tiny bay over a saddle in some rocks to a slight upward incline, deep in dewberries and ferns. At the top of this incline stood the three tall trees which he had seen from the shore, now taller and more noble in their graceful growth.

When he reached the tree the Phoenician found a small hollow in the centre of the grove which they made, and in the hollow a hut – the walls of wattles and mud, the roof thatched with dead ferns. He entered and stopped – breathless. On a stone table in the centre if the hut was the Cup – not of gold or of silver, but of crystal or perhaps of diamonds, for light brighter than that of the stars sparkled and glittered from a thousand facets on it. It was in the form of a chalice, and giving off its own dazzling rays, seemed not to be standing on the table, but to be supporting itself a little above the surface.

It was impossible for Eusebius now to reach and seize in greedy hands so magnificent a thing. He scarcely dared to look at it. Indeed, he turned his head aside, and in so doing saw that he was not alone in that place. Seated to one side of the stone table over which the Cup was suspended was an old man, clad in white robes and with a beard as white as his garments. The light of the Grail diminished and died. The Cup disappeared. The light with which it had illuminated the room was replaced by that muted light of the sun which seemed by comparison not light at all, but a merely lesser degree of darkness, lacking life and joy.

'It is gone,' cried Eusebius, stricken.

'No,' said the old man. 'It is not gone. It is only that you cannot see it.'

'Who are you?' asked the Phoenician.

'I am Joseph of Arimathea, who brought this Cup to this White Island. I am permitted to show it to those who seek it for the right reason. For what reason have you come in search of it, my friend?'

'That I might, having died, return to life by drinking from it,' said Eusebius. 'That I know is the virtue of the Cup – that he who drinks from it will never die.'

'No man will ever die,' said the old one. 'Man is immortal and that which is called death is only change. I must ask again, for what reason have you come in search of the Cup?'

'At first I sought it so that being dead, I could return to life, as I told you,' said Eusebius. 'Now I seek rather to learn the meaning of life and of its sister, death, for that which has no meaning has no value.' It seemed to him that the magic Cup – Grail – now glowed in outline before him above the table again.

'You have been much about the world,' said the old man. 'You have been through many perils and triumphs. You have seen Arthur in his ruined court and also the terrors of men during that time known as the Closing of the Ring. What meaning has all this for you? Or has it yet no meaning?'

'It has this meaning,' said Eusebius, 'that this life which we live here is of no worth or sense if it is spent to one's own purposes. That this same life has worth and value only if it is spent in the service of others – the greater the spending on others, the greater is its value. And here is a great mystery indeed, that that which is most precious to us, is valuable only in the degree in which we give it to others. And now at last I understand those puzzling words of Merlin that the mortality of men is the greatest of all wisdoms. For certainly it is the greatest of life's achievements to die having spent all of life for the benefit of others. There is no virtue greater thas that.'

'So He who first drank from that Cup taught us,' said

the one called Joseph of Arimathea. 'Drink now, knowing the true meaning of taking such a drink. But first reflect that having once drunk, your life belongs to others and not to yourself.'

Again the Cup glittered in a thousand lights before the Phoenician who, his wiles all gone now and his treasures forgotten, had come at last to the end of his quest. Eagerly he reached out his hand and seized the Cup. Such pain immediately flooded through his body that it was as if he had been drenched with fire. And yet he raised the Cup to his lips and drank deeply from it.

The Vikings waited three days, as they had been told, and then, when Eusebius had not returned from Avalon, they took counsel and left under the leadership of Vrilig, as the Phoenician had told them to do. From among the ferns of the island the Phoenician watched them go. No hut now stood in that glade between the three slender trees. There was no aged man and no Cup of Life called Grail. But the Phoenician was changed as he had been warned he would change, and he could no longer, with any joy, return to his comrades or to his own land, but was content to spend the rest of his life as a hermit and a healer of the hurts of his fellows in the mystic land of Lyonnesse, where earth and heaven are but the reflection one of the other.

(This ends the tale of Eusebius, the Phoenician, in the Chronicles of the West Vikings of Ostmond.)

There are now more than 500 Puffins
to choose from, and some of them
are described on the following pages.

Attar of the Ice Valley
Leonard Wibberley

The author says he wrote this book out of sheer
admiration for Neanderthal man. Admiration for his
courage – he tackled great cave bears, rhinoceros, and
wolves using only firesharpened wooden spears – and
for the art and ingenuity with which he decorated his
caves and made places of worship for the gods he
believed in.

Attar, the boy of this story, lives at a time when the
Ice Age is creeping down to his tribe, so he sets out to
find them food, refuge and shelter.

An absorbing book, accurate as possible in detail and
riveting in its tales of almost impossible feats of courage.
Especially for boys of 10 upwards.

Master Entrick
Michael Mott

One cold blustery night in 1754 young Robert Entrick,
as he rode home across the Lancashire Moors, suddenly
felt afraid, though it was easy on such a night to hear
things behind the wind. Then two figures on horseback
came up out of the darkness towards him. Someone
made a grab at his reins, someone struck him, and he
slipped sideways. . .
A few months later, having been brutally transported
to America where his new master was murdered by
Indians, Robert escaped. He was free, on his own, with
a few wet rags to wear, a short hoe, and a stolen canoe.
Here in the middle of America, with its woods full of
murderous savages, he was more shipwrecked than
Robinson Crusoe. And Robert Entrick, who had once
been afraid of riding alone in the dark, felt only a wave
of elation.

The Red Towers of Granada
Geoffrey Trease

It is a strange and terrible thing to listen to one's own
funeral service, to be sent away from one's home village
as a leper with clapper and bell, told never to enter an
inn or a market or a crowd again, never to walk barefoot
or speak to healthy people, not even one's own family.

Small wonder that young Robin of Westwood gave
his loyalty so freely to Solomon, the Jewish doctor who
saved him from this living death, and allowed him to
make a fresh start among his own people, even though
the Jews in England were suffering great hardships at
the time. They were forbidden to own land, lend money
or even practise as doctors, and then the final blow was
to fall : King Edward ordered all Jews to leave the
country.

The Spanish Letters
Mollie Hunter

'I will not save an English spy.' Jamie the Scots boy
shouted angrily, but he soon had to change his mind
when Macey explained what he was after. Two Spanish
agents had been reported in Edinburgh – a renegade
Scot called William Sample and a sinister, spiteful
creature known as 'the man in black' – and Macey was
out to foil their plans.

This thrilling tale of espionage also shows evidence of
much careful study of customs and sights and sounds
of sixteenth-century Edinburgh.

For readers of ten and over.

The Twenty-Two Letters
Clive King

Long ago, 1500 years before Christ was born, when King Minos of Crete still worshipped the bull, when the Eastern Mediterranean was divided into many unstable little states, and Egyptian writing was a sacred and secret cult, Resh the master builder lived in the city of Byblos with his three sons and his daughter.

Resh was very busy building a new palace for the King, but his three sons went off in different directions. All the time they were away their father and sister Beth were waiting anxiously for their safe return with the presents they should give the King on his Day of Offering. But despite the unheard-of way Aleph sent a message warning the King of his enemies approach, nothing could prevent the disaster which the strange man from the eastern land of Chaldea had foretold.

The Boy with the Bronze Axe
Kathleen Fidler

It looked like death for Kali and Brockan, who belonged to the Stone Age settlement of Skara in the Orkneys – they had gone out too far across the rocks, chipping off limpets with their stone axes, and were cut off by the returning tide.

Then a god came out of the sea to save them, or so they thought at first. But after all it was only a strange boy in a strange boat, and he carried an extraordinary and wonderfully sharp axe made from a substance he called bronze.

This is a fascinating and brilliantly imagined story of life in the Stone Age nearly 3,000 years ago in which Tenko the stranger with his bronze axe and his enquiring mind causes the same sort of upheaval and disagreement as the Industrial Revolution did nearer our own time.

For readers of nine and over.